T0290156

A FINE LINE

A FINE LINE

MARC SÉGUIN

TRANSLATED FROM THE FRENCH BY
KATHRYN GABINET-KROO

singular fiction, poetry, nonfiction, translation, drama, and graphic books

Library and Archives Canada Cataloguing in Publication

Title: A fine line / Marc Séguin ; translated from the French by Kathryn Gabinet-Kroo.
Other titles: Repentirs. English
Names: Séguin, Marc, 1970- author. | Gabinet-Kroo, Kathryn, 1953- translator.
Description: Translation of: Les Repentirs.
Identifiers: Canadiana (print) 20210221372 | Canadiana (ebook) 20210221607 |
ISBN 9781550969252 (softcover) | ISBN 9781550969269 (EPUB) |
ISBN 9781550969276 (Kindle) | ISBN 9781550969283 (PDF)
Classification: LCC PS8637.E476 R4613 2021 | DDC C843/.6—dc23

Original title: *Les repentirs* – Copyright © Éditions Québec Amérique inc, 2017.
  All rights reserved.
Translation copyright © Kathryn Gabinet-Kroo, 2021
Book and cover designed by Michael Callaghan
Cover artwork, "Portrait of Arielle Murphy," by Marc Séguin
Typeset in Bembo font at Moons of Jupiter Studios
Published by Exile Editions Ltd ~ www.ExileEditions.com
144483 Southgate Road 14 – GD, Holstein, Ontario, N0G 2A0
Printed and Bound in Canada by Gauvin

We acknowledge the financial support of the Government of Canada through the National
Translation Program for Book Publishing, an initiative of the Roadmap for Canada's
Official Languages 2013-2019: Education, Immigration, Communities, for our translation
activities.

We gratefully acknowledge the Canada Council for the Arts, the Government of Canada,
the Ontario Arts Council, and Ontario Creates for their support toward our publishing
activities.

Canadian sales representation: The Canadian Manda Group, 664 Annette Street,
Toronto ON M6S 2C8 www.mandagroup.com 416 516 0911

North American and international distribution, and U.S. sales:
Independent Publishers Group, 814 North Franklin Street,
Chicago IL 60610 www.ipgbook.com toll free: 1 800 888 4741

to

Arielle Murphy

ONE

She had said: "…first the cracks become crevices, which then become a ravine…"

That was a few years ago. I remember it like it was yesterday. We had been standing and waiting for the doors in front of us to open. An ordinary community centre that served as both gym and theatre. Beige and grey, decorated for the evening with bouquets of plastic flowers too beautiful to be real, white balloons, and satin bunting with fabric rosettes set three metres apart. She never finished her sentence. We went in, the people applauded and smiled too hard. The master of ceremonies, a callow stranger, shouted into the mike, "We welcome an extraordinary couple. She is extra and he is ordinary… Let's welcome our newlyweds, Arielle and Marc!" The audience laughed. It was normal.

That didn't bother me. I felt sorry for the guy. It did nothing but fuel my rage. And my hatred of the world. Normal since the beginning.

I got married for her. I couldn't say no to her.

That was before I truly understood the magnitude of lies. I've known about their usefulness since I was a little boy. Lying had kept me alive.

This was also before the commonplace deception of an outwardly honest and sensible life was revealed. I should have suspected. Arielle's mother was crazy, an unintelligent madwoman who licked stamps the way you would an ice cream cone, a woman who had made pig's feet stew every Saturday since 1971 and lasagna every Monday, and who watered the pavement and the sides of her clapboard house every Saturday except in winter.

She had a passion for products that killed spiders and other household insects, and spent weekday evenings watching soap operas on TV. To Arielle's mother, real life was an empty space. Filled by the lives of others. Every Christmas, she told the same story about pink grapefruit: "It was real special, pink grapefruit, back in my day… when I was little…"

I did not understand how the daughter had come from this woman.

I remember Arielle's breasts. Her breasts were the first thing that made me want to get married. The breasts that I had touched even before they appeared.

Today, despite the nightmares, and through the absences, I sometimes think about that. We were 14 and had found ourselves together, far from everyday life, one summer. Somewhat ashamed, neither of us spoke of it afterward, during the school year. We wanted to avoid being judged. By both sides. By pure chance, or perhaps not, we had ended up at the same summer camp, in Le Bic. We had smiled at each other, first out of embarrassment, but quickly the desire to be together took over. We'd been going to the same school for a number of years.

We were thrilled to be spending a week of our summer vacation, somewhere else, with a group of kids our age.

During the same hours. Far from home. She and I, we'd been serious for a long time. Even the adults sensed it.

Arielle would never have spoken of cracks and crevices when she was 14. Nothing and no one, at that age, could have predicted or guessed our future and its devastating trajectory. I now know that this is false: life is often an invisible track that we follow. And that sometimes guides us along the outer edges of awareness. Of our own awareness.

At the age of 14, a young woman already – she'd had her first period at 11, the summer our friend Med died – Arielle had a dense, confused, and unsettled inner life. Nothing serious, but far from the picture of tranquility that she hoped others saw. I also learned later in my life as a man that all women have unsettled, dense inner lives. While some allowed me into theirs, several preferred only to mention it. Others allowed me a glimpse of it in intimate moments.

With her, it was different. I knew we would go a long way. This girl would be part of my life no matter what. My existence depended on her.

A few months before we got married, I'd said, "Fuck, Arielle, if we're going to be in love with each other for a long time and make a life together, you're gonna to have to let me in, okay?"

I was sick of her tears and her therapies. I hated the fact that they'd become normal. Nothing serious, but I knew that, as always, the tears preceded the words.

"Talk to me, okay? *To me*. Look me in the eye. We're together, Ari."

That time, she had opened up and told me about her childhood, about her father who beat her mother, and how her whole family kept quiet so that the truth would never come out. An uncle with hands that reached too far. A first boyfriend at university who made the mistake of forcing sex on her. Had I known, I would have killed him.

Her eating disorders. The inner world that she maintained, telling herself that life was beautiful in spite of it all. Her self-respect. Her self-confidence. She who had tried to speak. No one believed her. And for what came later, even worse, no one would believe her. A string of culpabilities. A woman verging on normal. She, for whom words, to be both written and spoken, were a redemption. She, for whom the injuries – the blows and the marks they left, even if concealed – would one day serve her art.

"You can trust me. You don't have to use me to get back at other men."

We had discussed truths that day. We would go far.

So, about her breasts. At the age of 14. The first time. During that week at Le Bic. One evening, we found ourselves in a tent, biding our time while the counsellors were busy with the fire and marshmallows. All the signals had been sent. Follow the protocol.

I still don't know how it happened, but I bent over her, in the darkness, and our mouths touched. Inexpertly. An awkward first kiss. In an uncomfortable position, amidst the sleeping bags. Long seconds of euphoria. We caught our breath. Three times in a row. That was it.

By the fourth kiss, I had one hand between her sweater and her skin. A hand that worked its way upward. She let it happen. A bra. Arielle had hardly any bosom at 14. I remember having gently caressed the padding of her brassiere. And having imagined the rest. Later, around the campfire, she pressed herself against me. Her wool sweater was patterned with flowers.

Her entire world was unknown to me. An abyss.

Astonishing. Beautiful Arielle. I was so proud. We had made it to that point. I did feel a little guilty about having slid my hand up there, but she was proud too, like me. Later, she told me so. She could live a long time with such a memory. We thought we had become adults. It was also something that she herself had craved. "I wanted your hand on me so badly."

When we came home from summer camp, my friends asked how my week had been. They had heard about Arielle too. At that age, such news spread like wildfire.

Out of respect, I didn't discuss the French kissing. Not a word about her breasts. Such restraint only heightened the glory. It belonged to her and to me. To us. A source of pride. One more secret. A different one. One that was beautiful.

The roots we planted ran deep. It had begun when we were 11, with the death of Med, and had lasted until this point. For us, the deeper we delved into feelings, the more we found each other.

She and I, we began at the centre of the world. An infinite distance from here. Under the deepest of roots.

I don't know if it's inevitable in the real life of normal people, but I know that the closer we get to the abyss, the more solid it becomes. We were a quarry. We mined the tender silence of long years. We dug deep. Even when we lost sight of each other after high school, the echo still resonated up to the heavens.

She and I both went to the seminary, a private school that had only started accepting girls a decade earlier. The boys no longer took holy orders. The clientele had been enlightened and the young men went elsewhere. Faith and its folklore disappeared as well. Thought had been humanized with respect to this noticeable deficiency; first a few women, and suddenly girls had rights.

In elementary school, I never even dreamed that there were differences. Except when it came to the girls in my classes at school, girls with their rules of the game and natural affinities. Nothing had alerted me to the reality of women. My mother worked and had freed herself from certain conditioned reflexes, but it came at great sacrifice. For Arielle, the world was opening itself up.

We spent the five years of high school together. We lived side by side, phantom lovers. But never openly so. The week at Le Bic had clinched it. But only in secret. Far beneath the surface of the earth. We hoped for each other with all our might. Convinced by an innate certitude. A vibration. The kind that heralds a train or an earthquake.

I occasionally wondered if I had been obliged to love her. Where did this feeling come from? And especially: was it authentic? Despite my high-functioning autism, I could decipher feelings. Groundswells. Like the tidal waves that I saw – believed I saw – in the distance.

Over the years, I increasingly felt yearnings for her that existed nowhere else. I was fascinated, and surprised. Up to that point, I had believed myself impervious to human emotion.

I never truly felt empathy for anyone. Aside from my mother, Arielle, and a few stuffed animals that lulled me to sleep every night when I was a child. And certain insignificant objects, like a pillow, a sweater, a photo, or a dog that I ended up killing because he suffered from dysplasia and my mother hadn't had him euthanized because she couldn't afford to do so.

The dog has remained an intense memory. Of sadness, I presume. The nostalgia I felt had existed only before I put him down. No feeling at all once I'd shot him through the ear with my little .22 caliber. I had taken him near the bog where we used to go to catch frogs. On a leash. An ordinary walk. The rifle in a hockey bag. I had taken dog biscuits with me. To make amends.

He never had a clue. His name was Lou, a husky that I called Woofy. Lou slumped to the ground like a sack of potatoes. A single movement. Vertical drop. Dead. The blood ran from the other side of his head. Slow and dark. I watched for a few minutes. Calm. Fascinated by the end of life. The scene was more peaceful than I had imagined it would be, and the emotions were not those that I had feared. I expected something else. I had been certain that I would shed tears. Real ones. Only one had fallen. Finally. It made quite an impression on me.

I suspect that the tear had appeared before I pulled the trigger. Or maybe it was because of the pollen, or the dust.

I had to deal with the dog's body. Thinking ahead, I had packed a shovel along with the rifle, but the ground was too rocky. I dug a little, resigned. After a few minutes, I dragged Lou by his front paws, his head dangling, to the shallow hole and covered him with stones, grass, leaves and cattails. I remember telling myself that the next time I had to shoot a dog, I'd grab him by the hind legs; even with the fur rubbing the wrong way, against the ground, it would be easier.

On my way home, I ran into Arielle in front of her house.

"You okay?"

"Yeah, I just killed my dog."

Arielle said nothing more. Unruffled. She knew that I was telling the truth.

During our remaining years of high school, we kept each other at arm's length. I had believed that the summer-camp kisses would be enough to formalize our relationship. At age fourteen, I already knew that it took more than that. It was okay. We'd get there.

We understood the connections. Invisible and undeniable. The whole world knew that we'd end up together. It was written in the stars. Arielle and Marc. Marc and Arielle. Still had to make it to the end. Kill time until then.

My mother also added her two cents. Like a metronome, she'd asked me, "How's Arielle doing?" I told her that Arielle was a friend. A true friend. Everyone felt it. Never any pressure.

When my mother and Arielle saw each other, their feelings for each other were uncomplicated. Genuine. When we were younger, before high school, Arielle sometimes slept at my house on the weekend. In my room. Like a guy friend. We talked for hours in the evening and then on into the night. We looked at the moon and the stars and invented stories together. She loved it.

She was simply a part of our lives. The fact that I had a female friend reassured my mother. So accustomed was she to her son's energy. It made her feel good. I was happy for her.

It all changed one day at the end of summer 1981. Arielle got her period and the nature of our friendship was lost. She never again came to sleep at my house. I finally understood. Even if it took me years. I believed at first that it was because Med had died.

I know that I can comprehend very complex things in a fraction of a second. I was never too swift, however, when it came to the obvious. As for women, they know. And deal with it.

We saw each other at school. Our friends no longer teased us about the time we spent together. Occasionally, a new student would bring it up. Then everything would fall back into place. We were together. Even if the amorous impulse had not been defined, we figured it out.

Contrary to expectations, the feeling we shared was far beyond the customary. This was also part of the reason why we decided to get married in such a cheesy and predictable manner: to reassure our families, her slightly foolish mother, our friends and all the others. She and I had promised ourselves to each other long ago. Years earlier, we had said as much. All we had to do was tell the others – the family and a few friends and relatives – in a way that was easy to understand. And it had truly amused me to see all those people so reassured by our compliance with the standards of respectability.

One day, we were 16. Then 17. Arielle left to study somewhere else. She boarded at a sports-and-horsemanship college. I played hockey while she rode horses. English saddle. Dressage. Competition. We were separated because she loved to ride. I might have hated horses because of that. I didn't.

Separated for two years. Nothing dramatic. Promises, too, can span the ages. Sometimes vows don't hold up on their own. They need assistance. Especially during adolescence. I did not want to imagine her with another boy.

I missed her. With all my might, I yearned for her. With all my might, I pretended that I did not. More and more often, I found myself pretending.

This worried me. Because too frequently, when I strive to have feelings or to experience an emotion, I succeed. To protect myself, I wanted to stop loving her. I finally believed it. Against my better judgement.

It's an all too familiar situation: desiring the opposite of what we are in order to protect ourselves. Most often, it is through fear's crack that failures seep in.

I spent two years acting as if I no longer loved her. Repeating it to myself, day after day. Every hour. Until it worked. Then, one day, I didn't love her anymore. A May 23rd. We were 18. We cannot not love each other in the future tense. That is love's shortcoming: it requires the present.

Dreams eventually get worn down, even the loveliest of them, by dint of remaining too long in a state of hope.

She had come home for the summer. She's a woman, I remember thinking. Her body. Ahead of mine and ahead of life. At 18 years old, she already had the body to match her life as a woman. It was so long ago, that summer when we kissed for the first time, I thought, impressed.

We met each other on our high school's playing field. Early evening. It was hot. We always did like the swings in public parks. Swings had always been a link between us.

Merry-go-rounds, too, those rides that I spun so energetically, that she rode to challenge me, and that she clung to so as not to be ejected. When she climbed off, she staggered, dizzy as if she were drunk. I thought she was beautiful.

"See, Marc, how I feel when I want you to love me…" she'd said that evening.

Childhood memories that we carried into the adult world. It so happened that at that very spot, years later, I would ask her to love me forever.

"I'm at a different place, Ari."

That was the only fraction of truth I was able to speak on that evening of May 23rd. A confession. The beginning of concern. I remember the shock in her eyes. Dumbstruck. And the trembling that she struggled to control.

I envied her. Her feelings were much more appropriate and real and vast than mine. My whole body told me to cry out to her that I wanted to be with her. My whole brain screamed that I should turn my back on her, refuse to be at the mercy of my emotions. Because emotions were for other people. The weak. Not for me. I had known that for a long time. My condition. We weren't grown up yet.

It was with resignation that, one day, I decided to tell her everything. Long after we were married. Just like that, one morning, out of the blue. Confess all of it.

In a science-fiction future, many years later, I would come back from New York. Forsaking the life I'd been living somewhere else, without her. To find her again. For always.

But on that May night when we were 18, Arielle went back home alone, upset, shoulders slumped as she walked. Disappointed. I remember when she turned her back. I remember a lot about her back. And about her expectations. Especially about those. It was all clear to her. Us. Since we were little. We knew that our course had not been charted, but it was there, ahead of us. All planned out. Summoning us. The way a whirlwind pulls people into it.

We were also concerned about what would come after that summer. I was afraid. More than she was. I had always been afraid of time and distance. This time, I felt it: adult life was lying in wait for us. The life we could no longer keep at bay. No turning back.

We had already promised each other. She would go study elsewhere, and I would go far as well. We led parallel lives. Like two railway tracks. I was afraid. That was why the coward in me had decided to abandon and reject her.

The day after that evening, on May 24th, I broke my leg playing hockey. Fractured the tibia and fibula. Surgery. An orthopedist put everything back in place, using metal plates and screws. I was playing Elite. Midget AAA.

I spent eight weeks in bed. Thinking about fate. Questioning it. Trying to puzzle out a meaning. Feeding my fear. Telling myself that life makes corrections when we stray from who we are.

Sudden change of direction. Switching tracks. Like a train. Once again, invisible rails. Was it perhaps Med, my dead friend, trying to tell me something? I remember finding life strange and frightening for a few days. I began to listen and, as of that moment, to distrust signs of things to come. Because, as I told myself, they are everywhere. Perhaps I was not yet aware that things and time prevail.

I had the operation on the evening of the accident. They repaired my leg in orthopedic surgery. My dream of hockey, snuffed out. I didn't cry; I had always had a disconcerting ability to accept the circumstances of any inevitability.

Although disappointed and devastated, Arielle avoided detection and ignored visiting hours to come see me. They had given me something for the pain. Demerol, fed to me intravenously. I don't remember seeing her. My mother told me, the next day, that Arielle had paid me a visit. A vague memory of seeing them give each other a big hug in the corridor. It may also have been a dream. Wishful thinking.

Eight weeks of trying to understand and formulate a meaning for what had happened. That's just the way it is, I thought: the heavens are punishing me for what I've done. Eight weeks during which my thoughts became unbearable. Ever since then, I have detested the poisonous nature of my dreams.

It was also at that very moment that I really began to draw and write. A little to relieve my boredom and a lot to ease the guilt. Doesn't matter. It all began to make sense. Up to this point. Until today. Because from that, I constructed an emotional state and a full life.

Unbridled hours lay before me. A yearning for solitude, too. And a rage. I know that it was all there before. Dormant. Overnight, I turned off the radio, unable to bear it. It felt like an assault.

I started to read. My mother didn't read much but she had inherited a collection of books from her own mother. My grandmother, the daughter and wife of farmers. A strong woman. Without an education, and whose only window allowing her to see beyond herself and her daily life was reading. A refuge. Or an illusion.

"For so many women…" Arielle had said.

That was the summer when words entered into me. To come back out again only years later. I read everything that was stacked up in my mother's pitiful little wooden bookcase from Ikea. The books were arranged according to size, the little books with little books, the medium ones with medium ones, the big with the big. Shelved in ascending order.

When my mother died, that bookcase was the last piece of furniture I took apart and packed up in a box: the shelving and the books. Still organized according to format.

Dostoyevsky, Anne Hébert, Solzhenitsyn, Romain Gary, Marguerite Duras, Céline, Colette, Balzac, Malraux, Gide, Hemingway, the odd Michel Tremblay, a few plays, Marie-Claire Blais, Réjean Ducharme, Flaubert. The books all smelled of dust. The pages' edges had all yellowed. Oxidized. The ink itself survived. Arielle, later, admired this over-abundance of reading. She envied me.

"I can hardly believe you read so many millions of words in just eight weeks."

I had done the calculation: three million, one hundred and two thousand and 23 words. I read through the entire collection, that summer of the broken leg. The whole thing, one book after another. In their order of classification. If, in the middle of the day, I finished one, I mustered all my courage, slid out of bed on my butt, and hobbled on crutches to the living room. From there, leaning on the furniture, I stood, returned the book that was gripped between my teeth or held tightly against my back by my belt, took another one and returned to my room. My leg was immobilized, slightly bent at the knee, in a plaster cast all the way up to my groin. I arrived in a sweat, happy to be holding other worlds in my hands.

My only break from reading – because at a certain point my eyes began to sting – was drawing. On eight-and-a-half-by-eleven-inch paper. With lines, and holes punched to fit a three-ring binder. Lead pencil. Later, in a few weeks – like an omen – with ink.

It was also the only time in my life when I wrote poetry. A simple art, so truthful when it's set apart from a career and expectations. Lack of means. A complete collection. I believed myself a poet. I have read poetry every day since that year. Poets upset the symmetry; that's the only poetry worth its while.

I was going to disrupt the order. That much I knew.

I owe a great deal of my existence to illusions. My own, but also those of others. Sometimes the lies we tell ourselves become everyone else's reality.

It is also within this illusion, in Arielle's that is, that we fell back in love. A situation that was expected, and normal, at last. Injured, I had understood, and felt the need for conformity. Between willingness and atonement.

To this day, as a grown man, I still do not know the feeling of love. I have acted otherwise for all these years.

At the end of eight weeks, they removed the thigh-high cast and replaced it with a smaller one, which this time stopped just below my knee. With a plastic heel. I could slowly begin to put weight on my leg and walk. A tiny little leg, atrophied by its confinement.

The doctor's only instruction was to go to the threshold of pain, wait a few days and then try again. This, I understood. Physical pain was a fundamental part of me.

On my first day with the new cast, in mid-July, Arielle came to my house. She had followed my convalescence from a distance, with my mother's help. She wanted to mark the milestone. She had always been like that: caring.

She brought a gift: a pen and a little bottle of Pelikan ink. A real pen, made of metal, that you had to dip and load with ink in order to write. I never asked, but I suspect that my mother had told her that I was writing and drawing a lot, even if I was trying to hide it. This level of attention and empathy, which I for too long associated with women, amazed me. I was blown away. I hadn't seen it coming and it worried me that I'd had no clue.

Arielle didn't know it, but she had just turned my life upside down with something that cost $1.49. The earth, the sky, and the Universe had just opened up. I was going to be an artist. A chasm within me.

Obviously, I didn't tell a soul. Too fragile. Embarrassed by my vulnerability and fearful of revealing to others what I truly was. It takes a madman's courage to be an artist.

As the summer wound down in mid-August, I started to walk a bit. In a few days, Arielle would leave for her last year of college. Still far from here. From us. From intimations of us.

I myself would be finishing my last year of CEGEP in health sciences. A choice that had pleased my mother more than me. The truth is that before I began to draw, I was ignorant of my identity. I docilely followed paths drawn by others according to what they wanted. For me.

School had always been easy. Prior to university, I had never opened a school manual or a textbook. I was a model student and an athlete and accepted responsibility in all my student jobs: I had understood the system. The system was predictable. I earned good grades throughout my academic career. I had figured out the world of adults. With no effort at all. I could have settled for the minimum, but an inner voice was screaming at the top of its lungs. A voice that never shut up. I remember that the adult world had disappointed me. I would not be a part of it. Not for anything in the world.

The following year, my first at university, I began earnestly learning what it meant to be diligent, to make an effort.

Arielle's absence, that distance, which I did not acknowledge, drove me to surpass myself. I hated school as much as a fracture. I would have preferred amputation: living with the fiction for the rest of my life.

I handled the pain. I went on. Far away from her. During that first year in medicine, I spent more of my nights painting and drawing than I did studying.

A sense that I existed, sudden and searing.

One spring evening, at the end of that first year at university, my mother heard me. I didn't want her to speak. "Let me finish!" I wanted her to listen. Nothing more. Still paralyzed by the embarrassment of showing her my work, I found just enough courage to describe to her my life since Arielle had given me the pen and ink a few years earlier and the existence I'd experienced through my efforts to make art. She smiled and then suggested that I register in Concordia University's art program. She herself was employed by this prominent university. If I got accepted, I would not have to pay tuition. I put together a portfolio in a matter of days. Wrote letter of intention, too, in which I stated the urgency. To speak. To name.

The acceptance letter came a month later. I smiled, for once in my life. Naïve and deeply concerned. For all to see. It was my choice. As a child, I had learned to smile at the right moments, especially in photos, to make people think that I was normal.

This time, at the age of 20, it was a genuine smile. Like all whirlwinds. Sucked in by the void. The plummeting would be so beautiful. That emptiness, that hole that until now had proven me right.

I did the three years of the art program as faithfully as a priest. I was never even one minute late and I graduated with honours. I worked morning, noon and night. Non-stop. Every minute was a miracle. I discovered who I was. To the sounds of Leonard Cohen and Richard Desjardins, pressing "repeat." In my mother's unfinished basement, on top of a freezer that served as my worktable. That's where I experienced euphoria for the first time. Bent over the paper and canvas. Bowing humbly before the life I led.

The rest has been a series of trials and errors. One day, as I glanced back for a fraction of a second, I realized that people were calling me an artist. It was others who, once again, ended up saying the word. Stating the fact. They say that I am an artist. It sets everyone's mind at ease.

I saw Arielle again at the end of my first year in art school. She looked at what I had done and liked it. That meant everything to me. Without saying so, I sought her opinion. It was her absence that was giving me strength. Her breathing, and the breath that she had held longer than usual. Her eyes. One word.

One night, when I was a student, I had a vernissage and she said, "Have a wonderful evening." It was then, at that second, that I embarked on life.

Her silence about my paintings would slay me.

I still can't explain it, but she and I fervently believed that we had always been promised to each other. Impossible to describe without touching upon inevitability. And yet that was enough.

Over time, we became adults.

I spent three years' worth of days and nights secretly living just for her. A little for myself, of course, but in case of uncertainty, she was the one I clung to. And a bit to my mother too. But my mother gradually disappeared from the equation, replaced by another woman. In all the years up to now, I've never been anything but a one-woman man. Incapable of belonging to two.

Back then, even though Arielle and I had reconciled, we didn't see much of each other. She was studying literature. She'd given up riding for reading. Later, they would come back into our lives. Both of them.

Although we didn't see each other, or only infrequently, we waited and hoped for each other more and more.

For my part, nothing had been promised. It was more stringent than vows; our connection had been preordained. By the end of my third year of undergraduate studies, Arielle was all I thought about. She was in each breath I took. She haunted me.

She had begun to be present in every minute, every second, in every desire. I found it troubling. Until then, I had never needed anyone in order to exist. I recognized that she had once helped me, but I would have been able to handle the tragic consequences of that summer of 1981 without her. By taking a different path.

On December 19 of my last year in the university's art program, my mother died. In her sleep, probably from a stroke. Natural causes. I had come back home for the holidays. I was the one who found her that morning, peaceful, still in bed. Cold. I remember her forearm. I'd had the time to make myself a cup of coffee before I began to worry. I'd knocked on the door to her bedroom, thinking that maybe she had a cold or a fever and that illness explained her silence.

She was dead.

I saw a connection there. I always saw connections – even without feelings – between the joys and sorrows in my life. I always believed that these were all related. An accountability that I could not explain. Could my desire for Arielle have killed my mother? Nowhere to lay the blame. Reality. A smooth ride. Personal justice. Difficult to understand, this mystery called love. Connections that we fail to notice. Are there invisible equivalencies between all events in our lives?

I buried my mother. When I was just becoming a man. This woman whom I had reassured and protected since I was a child.

One Monday evening, three days after her death, I felt free. Carefree. Relieved, rather. No longer having to conceal things. My mother died in her sleep. The doctor who signed the death certificate didn't think an autopsy was necessary. I was 21 years old.

I'd thought that two women couldn't inhabit the same hours at the same time. A child's computation. Simple. One foot in the world of men and the other, somewhere else entirely.

I graduated in the spring, and the following summer, with the money from my inheritance and her insurance, I left for New York to do a Master of Arts at Columbia University. Columbia's fine reputation within academia had already reached us here in Montreal. I was accepted on the basis of several letters of recommendation and a portfolio full of harsh, violent images. And on the commitment of $100,000 in tuition. Prestige can be bought, and its upkeep requires constant attention. In those days, with a modicum of intelligence and ambition, a degree from Columbia guaranteed entry into the art market, the future and speculation.

There were a number of us who benefitted from this vogue. Trends are enigmatic, but they exist. Some invent them. While several young artists like me took part in this, the guarantee of longevity is not inscribed on a diploma. The contemporary art world had already belonged to financiers for a decade. Collectors, speculators and bankers had gained control of the market and of institutional thinking. The art market is manipulated, the most manipulated market in the world. Being part of it is easy. There are codes that you either accept or you don't. The art market's rules are not all that mysterious.

But making real art within their confines is quite an achievement.

I settled in Brooklyn and started living my life. Arielle came to see me twice during my first year there. Everything was easy with her. Simple. We weren't a couple, even though we loved each other, I think. I was easing into an emotion, a love that was not compulsory. Hence her difficulty picturing the future.

I was good only in the present.

A template for love is imposed on us very early on: be in a couple, go to sleep and get up together, have a house, plan a family, share projects, think of the future. More lies.

I had the beginnings of a career before graduating from Columbia. The galleries and the art community had decided that young artists would be the stars of contemporary art. I still have no idea how I managed to make it through that world and those years without going crazy or shattering my soul on illusions.

I did, however, fine-tune my loathing of humankind and my hatred of the world.

I visited all the big American and European cities when accompanying my works to exhibitions. I witnessed every vice and failing of the great "Free World." I was offered women, trips abroad, villas, drugs, money, weapons and cars. I pushed all the limits of my desires. From this I was able to invent myself. I said no a hundred times to serious people and their phony ideas about happiness. And I fought very hard against cynicism. Even when it was needed to survive.

That's when I learned that I lived on the fringes of human nature. I do not understand why I didn't kill myself. The stage was set. It would have been easy to believe that I was important and necessary.

I had affairs with American actresses and singers. Today, when they come to Montreal to make a movie or do a show, we still see each other. Kirsten, Scarlett, Jennifer, Lana. Hugely intelligent women, no matter what this world of images might say or publicize about them. The lack of intelligence comes from promoters, publicists, and people who write to entertain the masses. The economy triumphs in hackneyed phrases.

One day, a young woman from San Francisco managed to reach me via email. She knew my date of birth. Her message, which included pictures of herself, said that she had come to New York to give herself to me for a week. A birthday present. Utter nonsense. I was afraid. There were other such stories. My revulsion increased tenfold.

So I began to write my first novel. To reconnect, by hook or by crook, to my happy memory of reading throughout the year of the broken leg. I needed signposts. With all due respect to good intentions, neither love nor its offshoots provided any support.

I began to silently implore my dead mother to help me carry on. "Help me, Mom, please," I begged. I had given her a great deal of reassurance when she was alive, so I asked, for myself this time.

I know that when I was a child, she had given her all as a mother, but this was something else. I couldn't ask Arielle. I had to remain cautious. Avoid worrying her. Arielle, my sanctuary.

Better to ask the dead. It proved to be an easier solution than speaking to the living. Live people are so complicated.

My mother became a ghost. First, in the figurative sense. As in the way we appeal to the heavens with a prayer or a wish. Then one day, in broad daylight, she appeared. Translucent. Right in front of me. That first time, she didn't speak, although I felt her thoughts. One morning, when I was still comfortably lying in bed and feeling lazy, I had a daydream as I stared wide-eyed at the ceiling. She was at the foot of the bed, standing and looking at me. It seemed quite normal. Only natural.

I never believed in ghosts. I'm more the type who made fun of people for whom they were real. I always thought that feeble minds invented them to make themselves more interesting. Especially the people who really believed in them. They're like people who read their horoscope and insist on seeing a harmony of connections where there would otherwise be none.

It's so easy to believe in magic when daily life is utterly ordinary. From the impulse to make art, I had learned the need to magnify our lives. Survival demands it. We need this other world. It's part of who we are. Compensation for what we lack.

I still haven't shed a tear since my mother's death. How strange, I'd thought at the time. I should have had the appropriate emotion. It's always on display; it seems to be required of normal folk. That was the first thing I had said to her that morning: "Forgive me for not crying."

I definitely quashed a surge of feelings when her wooden casket entered the incinerator on some kind of conveyor belt equipped with metal rollers. A huge, heavy automatic door, also made of metal, was shut. Maybe that was when I felt something. It certainly made an impression. Her body would be gone forever. According to her wishes: convinced that she would die from a disease like cancer, she wanted all the goddamn cells that had killed her to burn, expire and disappear. She had plotted her revenge. I found that beautiful.

I remember a great sound of rushing wind. Through the little window in the iron door, flames. That was it. The rest was unbeknownst to me. An employee would wait, and once the oven had cooled, he would collect the ashes. I pictured him with a broom. Or maybe some kind of vacuum cleaner?

The next day, I was given an urn. The least unsightly of the soulless containers they'd shown me. I had chosen one with a flower — an embossed white rose — since the two of us had always loved flowers. Engraved with her name and the dates.

I still have it. The urn is sealed on the bottom with a screw. My mother's ashes are inside, in a plastic bag. Hence making these ghostly sightings in which she still had a body even more disturbing.

I never told a soul about it, until today. Because I ended up getting used to it. Her appearances, although surreal, were so frequent that they became normal. The first few times, I was startled. Scared. Especially when I sensed her presence, caught a glimpse of her in a mirror or in the reflection of a window. At night, it had sometimes sent a shiver down my spine. I was happy to have feelings at last.

"Mom, enough, please! You give me a heart attack every time you show up."

"Well, how do you want me to make an appearance?"

"Let me call you, it'll be simpler that way."

From then on, everything was easier. I made sure that no one was in the room, the studio or the house. People would have been afraid. I owe a lot to my dead mother. She was responsible for most of the ideas for the series of paintings, sculptures, and other projects that I did during my first years as an artist.

It was also during this ghost-mother period that Arielle and I became a real couple. No connection between the two. I have always hated Freudian psychology. I had been managing the differences between the roles played by women in my life for a long time. No ambiguity between the one that I would love and all the others. Even if it seemed suspicious, one had never replaced the other. A combination of circumstances.

I would soon return to Canada, and after years of high winds I calmed down, taken to task by my origins. And by her. By Arielle.

Probably also by a desire to leave my mark. My artwork was no longer enough. In the end, it wouldn't have provided enough of a guarantee. I signed my work and then to the right of my name, I put the year. Worried about time. Plagued by its hurried passing, by how quickly it flies. Time rushing forward. For a long time, ever since my friend Med died in 1981, I had been obsessed with keeping track of the signs we leave behind, with those we try to escape and with those we plant along the way. I think that's another reason why I became a painter. For painters, pasts are physical things.

I often pictured myself as an immigrant, with my need to pull up stakes and put down roots somewhere new.

And with the traces that we leave.

And with those that we do not.

I couldn't conceive of the notion that we leave no nicks or notches along the way. I liked indentations a lot, like the ones left on the skin by a bra strap or the elastic waist of a pair of pants. One day, Arielle had lain down on top of me. I liked to feel her weight on my body. It reassured and soothed me. She had kept her bra on and when she got up, she had one of my shirt buttons imprinted on the top of her left breast. I had run my finger over the indentations and smiled. I had come between her breasts, on her bra. It was still damp an hour later. Simone Pérèle. The letters SP stitched into the fabric in pink. 34C. Arielle Murphy. "Sarielle Purphy," I'd said with a smile as I touched her lace. She had made a sound of contentment and her eyes were filled with love.

I adored the smell of my sperm on her. Somewhere between black truffles and chlorine. The odour of a man and the scent of the wild. Like being anchored. By way of her perfume. She was mine. I had this need, this little need, from time to time, to be an animal. To be a living thing. She knew it and was happy and secure with this state of affairs. I don't know why. A need for human tenderness and human violence all at once. "Take me, Marc, take me hard…"

I was learning to be alive.

It was at my mother's funeral that I learned how much courage I would need to be part of a couple. A clear and sudden reality. I don't know why, but it seemed like all the events in my life had to equal out. A shortage – a surplus. A joy – a sorrow. Good news – and bad.

It's a fact that defies logic. Why this need for a tightrope walker's perfect balance? Arielle was born at the end of September, making her a Libra and her sign – the balance scales. For her, it made sense, but for me?

I dug deep to see if it was a wish I'd made when I was younger. The kind that comes true. I have always been afraid of what I wished for.

How could I have thought that my life would be more meaningful like that? With such expectations? After the clouds, a silver lining would appear. After too many happy moments, I dreaded the storm. For years, I preferred to stay in the middle. I avoided overly intense emotions so as not to provoke the others – the ones that hurt.

I loathe people who paraphrase Lavoisier's law, saying: "Nothing is lost, nothing is created." I am proof to the contrary. Looking around me, I see that despite the apparent loveliness, all – *all* – is lost.

I was never really concerned about my emotional state, other than pretending that I actually had one in order to reassure other people. Especially in order to put them at ease. Making sure that everything seemed to be in order. My lack of feelings was normal for me; I'd never known anything else. I'm colour-blind as well, and people are fascinated by the fact that I'm a painter.

I never saw my lack of emotion as a problem. But I realized that for others, it was. And for some it was even a cause for alarm. I had thus learned as a little boy to act sad, happy, disappointed, jittery, envious, possessive, affectionate. Acted out all the other states of mind, all the moods that contribute to the magnificence of human lives.

I had learned to display the expected states. To inspire confidence in others. To create the illusion. I was well aware of the need to do so. I had to allay people's fears about my nature. So that they wouldn't worry. So that they would never worry.

And so I learned to perform all the emotions and all the feelings. To guess, predict and imitate what people expected.

I spent long hours and a great deal of time in solitude, identifying and finding the best reactions for each mental state. As long as I was alone, I was free. It was only in social situations, and in a few intimate relationships, that I had to invent myself. I was very proud, at first, when it worked.

One day, I got used to it. I stopped talking – it was easier like that – and I became a great listener. I persisted in my unsociability, listening to others with their modern and unbridled need to talk incessantly. Many, in trying to define themselves, suffer the misconception that they exist when they talk. Truth is, all these people who yammer on about themselves bore me shitless. They're useless, in my opinion. They stand in front of the mirror and scream their existence at the top of their lungs.

I was greatly admired for my ability to empathize. To say only a few words at a time, and especially to see through people. I had no choice. My survival was founded on understanding the other and knowing how to behave in an interpersonal relationship. No one ever saw my distress. No one noticed the distancing from reality. The crevice. Except for Arielle.

Instead, they admired my humanity and the emotional intelligence I was able to fake.

I had to learn to read people. It was reading and the words that helped me the most – great writers know how to invent realities, and we believe in them.

I depended heavily on memory to get me to this point. My ghost-mother still helps, of course, but it's thanks to my memories that I slowly learned to love. At least to get close to it. Against my better judgement. By believing that love was an invention.

Reading body language can also help with mimicry. Sparkling eyes do not lie. What is said with sparkling eyes is different from what is said with vacant ones. There is always a moment, one precise second, when a promise can be made. Regardless of the immensity or the indecency, the truth or the lie, there are pledges that move things forward.

Making art saved me. Because it is like nothing else. Creating has immunity from social codes. Especially when it comes to painting. Far from words, particularly the ones used to name, speak and characterize. Far from the expectations of a language that diminishes us all.

Painting was the thing closest to my way of thinking: an unpredictable sequence of affirmations – existences – and a leap into the future of what we already are. An unsettling concern. A contradictory world.

Arielle was the only person I really talked to about it. Arielle, the woman of Arts and Letters. Who also did theatre. But she remained dependent on and a prisoner of the language of words. The words of others.

She wrote every day. Quietly, not making a big show of it. Able to describe with precision the intimate details, the nooks and crannies and depths of her thoughts.

One night in New York, as we were making love, my ghost-mother had appeared in the room. Arielle was straddling me, and there stood my mother behind her, at the foot of the bed. "Go away!" I'd begged her. I'd said it out loud.

"What'd you say?"

"Nothing, nothing, just that I wish I could make time stand still," I'd whispered.

My mother had disappeared.

But Arielle was worried. I knew it by the look in her eyes.

I had ejaculated.

I was lying down, her head on my left arm. Our breathing slowed. Our bodies too. Contented.

"Arielle…?"

She put her hand on my penis in sign of response. Such warmth. I could have spent the rest of my life like that. I said, "I'm coming back home… I'd like us to live together. You're the most beautiful woman in the world."

And that's how I came back to Canada. Just after an orgasm.

Tears, on my chest. She raised her head to kiss me. Her eyes were smeared with mascara. Her lips tasted of salt.

"Stop bawling, you're getting on my nerves! If you don't stop, I'm not coming back." I had to manage the discomfort. I liked it a lot when she cried. I believe that I was happy.

It's probably the one event in my life that came the closest to a romantic desire. Even if I knew that I was doing it for her.

Since that time, I've been fascinated by love. I wanted to believe that it was a real feeling. I wanted to get close to it, even though up until today, as I now know, I have never managed to let myself be completely loved. By anyone, not even by Arielle, with whom I was going to build a life. Our hearts set on each other. No, I never managed to let myself be loved, although I tried as hard as I could. In earnest.

I wanted so badly to let myself be loved. To feel that emotion. It had seemed possible, those first years. I had come back from the U.S. We moved in together, in a townhouse. In a nice neighbourhood in Montreal. From the outside, everything seemed real.

I fought an internal battle against my hatred of others. After all that time, New York had exhausted my supply of compassion. City of madmen. It's the most demanding place in the world. Blink your eyes, and you've already fallen behind. Although I had initially been fascinated by its candour and its clamouring, within a few years, it was silence that I craved. New York is also the most autistic place in the world. It wears a life down. Cult of personality, too. A place where it's easy and common to mistake an empty clown with attention deficit disorder for a terribly conscientious artist. Sad statement about a civilization that invented narcissism and its technology.

In New York, it's customary to believe that the art made for museums, money, and the market is superior. But for me, the creative act is not linked to such codes; I've had them all and was disappointed. Back rooms can be deceiving.

The subject of the last series of works I'd painted in Brooklyn was the *repentir*. The French word *repentir* means remorse or repentance, but in art history the *repentir* – or in English, the pentimento – is a portion of a painting that is covered over or repainted during its creation or even long after its completion, the purpose being to alter the meaning.

My series included portraits of men and women who'd been tried and convicted of murder. I modified them by erasing part of the face with turpentine and then painting over it. The visible trace of the pentimento revealed more than the certitude and its intention. I showed the intention.

Sometimes, painted light is more accurate and more beautiful than the real thing. Embellishing our humdrum lives. Existing in this voluntary act.

Returning to Arielle, to Montreal, had seemed normal. Especially the need for genuine love, which I was beginning to recognize. To comprehend. At first, I'd been a little nervous about the feeling. It was as if it wanted to exist. On the one hand, I rejoiced in it and on the other, I trembled at the thought. Love is an emotional state that I did not trust and one that I still guard myself against. I had promised myself that no one would ever convince me to let myself be loved.

My mother was never really a ghost. I knew that. But I adored the idea of making her appear, like a consciousness. The first. The one I had protected. From myself. Especially from myself. I began to look elsewhere for ideas.

I was far from being crazy, but I could make any and all believe that I was. Knowing perfectly well that even if it passes through a crack like light or a garter snake, it is sometimes preferable to withhold the truth.

Often, on peaceful, unhurried evenings, Arielle read to me. I liked listening to her. I thought of a thousand things all at once. Sometimes, too, when she took a little break, I would kiss her skin somewhere – a knee, an arm, her belly – or I would tell her I loved her. I caressed her thighs, her cheeks, and her eyes insisted. Our kisses lasted for minutes on end. Our bodies discovered each other. Often, we went on to make love. I always chose a moment when she least expected it. I know she liked that.

This too was learned. All my desires stemmed from hers.

Yet I did give myself real opportunities. I wanted to have emotions, true ones. I prayed for anything that might help. The way you put all your hopes in the ultimate reality of beautiful todays. The kind that turn into memories. I remember once, when we were playing a favourite game of challenging each other by asking questions that we had to answer, I was touched by a moment:

"What's your favourite story from when you were a kid?"

"A fable," she'd said. And my entire body had the urge to take her right then and there. I'm crazy about fables. I had lifted up her dress without asking any questions and pushed her back against the wall. Taken standing up. In my arms, her legs around my waist, gripping tightly. Me, giving great, deep thrusts. Beautiful, loving ferocity. A few minutes later, she went back to sit on the sofa with her knees curled up against her chest and sperm running between her thighs and onto her dress, paying it no heed, and she calmly told me the fable.

It was the story of a man, deeply in love with a magnificent woman. Wanting to prove his love for her, he had asked her what she desired most in the world. "Your mother's heart," the woman had answered. The man loved his mother a great deal and he told her of his lover's unreasonable demand.

His lover had promised him eternal love if he brought her the heart. The mother, whose love for her son knew no bounds, agreed that he could take her heart. He tore it from her body and thus she died. The man hurried to take the bleeding heart to his beloved. He ran very fast. Along the way, he stumbled and the heart fell to the foot of a cliff. The man climbed down to the bottom of the ravine and retrieved the heart. No sooner had he gotten back on the path but he heard his mother's voice coming from the heart. She said, "Tell me that you did not hurt yourself, my child."

We didn't discuss it. It had nothing to do with the psychology of mother-son-lover relationships. No psychoanalysis or Oedipus here either. We were a million miles from that. Arielle and I, we existed somewhere else. Her fable obsessed me for weeks. It had come out of the blue. I found it beautiful. I occasionally managed to believe, or at least to hope, that real feelings would one day be mine. Feelings are like prayers, I thought: if you believe in them strongly enough, you might just be content with that. Such moments became critical. Like a life that shatters, as well it should.

And so I let the months and years go by, secretly waiting. I built myself a life of façades: a house, a car, a future. Alone one sleepless night, I caught myself imagining growing old with her: the slow time of small gestures. The chairs that become important. The herbal teas. The silences.

It consoled me a bit. Arielle and I had sometimes longed to have a family, a continuation. To do things properly. I tried very hard to believe in all of it. To be a man in love. A normal citizen. I played the part. I fulfilled all the conditions.

With panache. I was convinced that by acting out all these emotional states, they would end up being real. Every so often, when I wanted to be sad, I was.

I tried very hard to take human form. With faith and diligence. I met all the requirements for social success. People believed me. This is too easy, I remember thinking. I had also learned to put on a sincere, self-conscious smile. People found me charming. Yet the last time I truly smiled at someone, it was at her, when I was 11 years old. Since then, an abyss.

The years passed. People believed in me more and more. I reassured folks. About their humanity. My own eluded me.

I had as much soul as a lightning rod.

I had been back in Quebec for a few months. We had moved in together. Arielle was teaching as a lecturer in literature at the university and the National Theatre School. She was writing a great deal. She was talented. She wasn't published yet but that would come. She sometimes had me read her texts. I admired her work, truly. That, I was able to do. Words had a power over me. I was sensitive to them.

"So, what do you say?"

"You really want to know?"

"Yes."

I was merciless; I gave no quarter. That's the way it is with those I've decided to love. I'm honest. No lying for sentimentality's sake, only the facts. She cried, again. But I'd been accustomed to tears for ages. I told her the truth: too many adverbs, your mother would never talk like that, your conjugations are mixed up, you used the wrong past tense, it's further in the past than the imperfect you used in the scene you're describing. She was quiet for a few seconds, then cried and thought herself a hack. That evening, she came back with her text, which was a hundred times better. "Check this out, I've got it," she said.

Upon occasion, I learned a lot through her as well. Arielle had an emotional intelligence that boggled the mind. She was light years ahead of me.

I'd said, "You know that I like writing... Sometimes, with the humblest of authors, it becomes like painting – you can always go back over it, make corrections and change things. When you think it's done, you have to start over. Again. And then again."

"Lazy writers write only for themselves," she said. "They don't give a damn about social survival."

In all forms of art, what you want to say must be clear. Then you have to search through a thousand sentences to find the one that will say it best.

"I love you."

"Me too, I love you, Ari."

It was close to the truth. Even if I wasn't convinced, I wanted it to be true. Sometimes that's enough. Even if such wishes are nothing but partial realities. It was better than nothing, I told myself.

There were days when I detested my optimism.

"Your tears don't scare me."

I was lying. I pretended that they didn't, but I was afraid. While to me, crying was a largely unfamiliar reaction, I had learned that it represented sadness or pain in others. Then one day, I understood that it was also a safety valve. It would have helped if I'd known this a little earlier. It would have made what came later so much easier.

"C'mon."

We went out. June. I had returned for good. The same park we'd visited when we were 18, the time that I'd abandoned her. Side by side on the swings, the sound of metal. I pulled my legs under me when the swing carried me backwards and stretched them straight in front of me when it began to carry me forward. I gripped the chains with all the strength in my hands. The wind against my skin. I dreamed of doing a full circle. And another, until there were no more chains.

"Arielle, it's simple, okay, I'd like to spend the rest of my life with you... I'm not good at proposals, but this is one."

Coming back wasn't enough. She wanted more. I could feel it.

She didn't say anything. She pushed with all her might, swinging even higher than me. I thought she wanted to sail into the sky. It was beautiful and violent. I remember being afraid. This was the most beautiful woman in the world. I stopped swinging for several seconds to watch her. She stopped fueling her momentum and sat immobile with her legs crossed under the wooden seat. She slowed as the movement wound down. I glanced at her. Her tears had begun to dry, leaving horizontal white traces on her temples. Like when she cried, lying on her back in bed.

When the swing came to a halt, she smiled. Still sitting, we turned to face each other, and she took my hand.

"Okay, Marc."

We decided to get married. More for her than for me. Which wasn't saying much. It made no difference to me one way or the other.

We could have had the biggest ceremony in the world, like people who marry for and before others. Anywhere on the planet. I had the liberty afforded by unlimited means, thanks to my money.

We chose to do it in our home town. At a community centre. I thought it made perfect sense. Imitating real life. The kind normal people led. What they call the "good life," for want of something better. There are rules to be respected if we want people to believe us. That much I knew.

I believe, today, that I truly loved Arielle Murphy. I'm not certain but I had a reasonable suspicion that I did. I am convinced, however, that I never did allow myself to be loved. Still not capable of that, and yet I grew to manhood long ago. Obstacles stood in the way of all my desires. I was never able to surrender myself to emotion. I continued to pretend. So that I wouldn't frighten her. So that she wouldn't feel guilty. So that she wouldn't cry too much. So that she wouldn't be disappointed. So that she wouldn't regret her life. So that she wouldn't hate me. That was my responsibility. It was a part of us. I kept us together. Above all else.

Above the abyss.

Art continued to compensate for all the normal sensitivities from which I was excluded. By proxy, and through the existence of others, I forged my own life. Years dedicated to creation. The invisible thread that kept my life in a safe place. A fortress, to protect me from myself.

"You tell a lot of stories, Marc."

We were lying in bed together in the middle of the afternoon. Her comment had struck a chord. That was my daily life, a fact that I could never acknowledge. I was too drawn into the darkness of living life, into its cries and whispers. I wish I could have just been normal.

A thousand times, I longed to be a labourer, with a forty-hour work week, three weeks of vacation a year, a simple tax return and a street address. Finding a reassuring meaning in the hours of TV shows and their illusions, believing in them, and then drinking a few shots of whiskey each week to choke down reality. A life lived vicariously.

I tried, especially with the booze. I tried drinking to understand and to keep going. I tried in vain. I don't like drunkenness. It's duplicitous, an assault of ecstasies and evasions. Committed against yourself.

I kept painting, writing, making movies and doing a ton of other stuff that I never talked about. In a holding pattern. Waiting, always waiting. Loyal love. Sometimes I picture myself as a serial killer. A terrorist. Slaughtering the innocent. Forcing a meaning. Believing in it. And calculating life through subtraction. Eventually, there are fewer years left than there were at the beginning.

I always smiled at the right moment. With great optimism. It's crazy the way people believed me. I occasionally wonder if other people do the same thing. There are so few of us. I could pick them out with confidence, anywhere I go. We'd send each other a signal. I often meet people in whom I sense the same emptiness.

I gave up the search for truth the day I understood that it provides no release. All ideas have their weaknesses. Nothing is infallible. Especially firm beliefs.

Sometimes I still believe in love, every now and then. Because of her. Fact or fiction? I couldn't care less. I'm inclined to believe in it, even though I'm wary of this impossible feeling. A doubt remains. I wouldn't be the first. So I acted as if I were truly in love. No one noticed the difference. No one would.

"You know that I love you, don't you?"

I always said yes. It's more effective. I detest deception. During the festivities that surround every New Year's Day, I pretended to believe in the promises and good wishes. In reality, I delighted in crossing another year off my life. Finally, one less to go.

And one more, added seamlessly. Everything was normal. People were not concerned. They believed me. They thought I had emotions, desires, a career, even certain values. Some thought that I loved a woman. Some considered me to be intelligent and sensitive. And all the while, I counted the hours down like years, doing a million little things to kill time. Sighs. An hourglass. A rosary. A train that passes.

"…first the cracks become crevices, and they become a ravine…"

Her story about cracks had captured my attention, just before we went into the reception hall at our wedding. Don't know why, but it made me think about the summer of 1981, when we were 11. The first visible fracture.

Maybe she knew. I'd thought I could hide it from her. I never believed in goodness, but Arielle bore a grace that transcended goodness. First a crack: mine, and it was a deep one. Never did become a crevice, even though it hid an entire world. I would have liked for her to tell me that she knew about everything.

One night, she said, "I know why...all your images... your work...your made-up stories... You have an endless need to be loved by the world. You're a bottomless pit, Marc."

Beautiful Arielle. Either we dealt with that notion, or I smiled and carried on as usual. She came over to kiss me. At varying levels, both literally and figuratively. I preferred living out that idea to showing her who I really was. I pretended that I'd been unmasked and that my feelings had been revealed. The evidence proves otherwise. Smiling, I responded, "Aw, no, you dummy. All that is just so you'll love me. You do know that I'm only with you for your pecan pie, right?"

I had long believed that I would make my life with the first woman to offer me a pecan pie. We were at a restaurant in New York during my university years, when we were in our early twenties. The waitress had mixed up our desserts and Arielle had pushed her plate toward me. I'd found that lovely. My prophesy.

I don't know where the road went after that, or even if there was one. I would have liked more books and the entire history of Painting to tell me. To help me. More years. Centuries that I did not have.

I liked the idea that she understood me.

"You're right, Ari, I am a bottomless pit. Thanks for the pecan pie, I love you."

She had told the truth and I had told the truth. For once. A portion of the truth. My only claim to fame is that no person has ever managed to reach me. Everyone dies along the way.

Forget mountaineering and exploring the cosmos, oceans, and mountains. These are little vanities. Continents and summits are boring; our interest is captured by the extreme limits that are reached. As for chasms, no flags proclaim their conquest. Our deepest self is so very far away.

I like painting portraits. And then erasing them. Keeping nothing but anonymous traces. That which was. Like a memory. There is often more certainty in disappearance than in the state of existence. Recognizing yourself from time to time is only one level of the self. I might be more useful dead than alive. We'll have to see. I didn't want Arielle, with her open and honest nature, to be deceived.

"Y'know, the idea for your second novel that you told me about?" she asked. "Why does the man kill the woman he loves? How could you have thought of making him do that?"

"Ari, it's not something I made up, it really happened."

She smiled, still somewhat worried. I have this way of not completely dispelling doubt when I answer, without being serious. Anyway, the truth, in the majority of cases that concern me, is impossible to believe.

We did talk seriously sometimes. More or less the average amount, I've since learned.

In general, Arielle and I lived a daily life with few surprises. Although I sometimes shut myself away in the studio for days or weeks, living in vast galaxies of creation, we led a normal life whenever I returned to her. That was, in fact, what worried me. Because the states into which I descended to make art were not human. And that became increasingly troubling. Sometimes, I was someone else. Often, I was someone else. A part of me, repainted.

At her funeral, I told the people only what they wanted to hear. I avoided all the rest. I maintained standards of grief and hope. With feelings of general acceptance. And a few tears, muffled sounds, and silences. I admitted to the pain, the love, the sweetness, the beauty and rage and violence, again, that her absence had wrought. I put great emphasis on how much I missed her. I painted her portrait.

At the end of the ceremony, I said, "You know, Arielle, the stories that I tell…like our story, they don't come from some other place."

She was buried late on Thursday morning, November 8, 2007.

TWO

Summer 1981.

I had turned 11 in March. An age when I was happy. It was coming to an end.

Before going to bed, even during the week, we had a ritual: I would lay my head on my mother's lap as she read me a few pages from the books she devoured each evening as she sat on the living room sofa. My mother, unlike Arielle's, never watched television. I greatly admired her for that.

It was, for me, the beginning of a curious age and I was eager to distance myself from childhood. A calm, orderly suburban life. A good school and friends. It was a time when newspapers were still delivered at the end of the day. I had the biggest paper route in the city, 81 houses.

Only on Saturday was there morning delivery. The rest of the week, I delivered late in the afternoon after school. No Sunday edition. I also had to "collect" from my customers every two weeks, going door to door with a notebook, like a calendar, and punching the weeks paid. Thursday evenings. Most of the people weren't at home. I hated people who weren't at home. They messed up my system of accounts and tips. It made me furious when things I'd scheduled deviated from the prescribed order.

Back then, people did their grocery shopping on Thursday evening or on Saturday. My mother had bought a house in a new development. The early days of urban sprawl. The neighbourhood was being built on a large piece of recently rezoned farmland that had belonged to a group of nuns, thereby adding to their wealth. If only the good sisters could have guessed at the drama that would play out in their former home. They would have prayed very hard to drive the evil from their land.

Real estate developers built housing projects there and sold the dream. A few months later, Mark David Chapman would assassinate John Lennon in New York. The crazies often kill those who pretend to be naïve. You can count on the crazies. They're dependable.

There was a lot of space between the houses. We lived near a sand quarry that was still operational, a small river, actually more of a creek, and the railroad tracks. Tracks where someone – a child – would die that summer of 1981.

A perfect suburban neighbourhood for raising a family. Lovely homes with greenery, paths for cycling and cross-country skiing, public parks, and schools. Basic promises for living within a community.

A bicycle made this neighbourhood the most wonderful playground for a boy. I know that now. I was in Grade 5 and had the new bike I'd received for my 11th birthday. Back in March.

My mother was not a wealthy woman. Her earnings were satisfactory for our survival. With some careful spending, she found a way for us to live happily, as if we were financially secure. Taking a few liberties.

A grey, five-speed *Free Spirit* two-wheeler. The snow had taken its time disappearing that spring. My mother didn't want me to go out until it had all melted. I couldn't understand her logic. And once it had finally gone, I pedalled in mud for weeks. I traced deep furrows into our beautiful lawn. I didn't want to wait. Could not wait. So I took advantage of the time before she came home from work.

I remember that the marks had remained there all summer, until school began in September. Some of the lines were long and parallel, like railroad tracks. Sometimes I put branches across them to make it look like real ones.

That spring, my schoolmates and I headed off to magical destinations on our bicycles. The quarry, the train tracks, the golf course, the Perrette convenience store. Hanging around. The streets at night. The arena. The kind of weeks we dreamed of. Summer nights, when at our age we stayed outside as long as possible, gave rise to indescribable feelings. Echoing freedom.

Samuel, the shyest of my friends despite his great size, had heard talk of a frog pond along the road to the sandpit. Luc, who had an older brother, knew of a hill that you could pedal down at full speed and where a big mound of dirt propelled you up into the air, a jump after which few riders managed to land without crashing. He knew about the train tracks, too. He said that his brother went there a lot. The CN railway.

From my house, in the evening and early in the morning, I could hear the bells at the railroad crossing. Always at the same time, even when the time changed in the spring and fall. A rapid *ding-ding-ding-ding-ding* that I mimicked by banging a spoon on a metal mixing bowl. It drove my mother crazy, but it made me smile. Proud that I had gotten to her. Ever the good sport, she joked that she was going to do the same thing, only this time with the bowl on my head so that I would understand just how much it irritated her.

All summer long, I would go outside when the bells clanged in the evening, even if we were in the middle of dinner. My mother rolled her eyes but accepted it, swayed by my sense of discipline. For me, it was an obsession.

From the street in front of the house, I could see the locomotives appearing and crossing the road, and I counted the railroad cars. For an 11-year-old, a real train is an enticement. A magnet. A reality greater than nature. A whirlwind.

"One hundred and three," I'd shout, exhilarated when there was a long convoy. At other times: "Seventy-one," I'd say, almost disappointed. And then I'd go back inside the house.

My mother repeated incessantly that I must never go play near the tracks.

"No, Mom, and anyway, I'm afraid of trains."

That was the first deliberate lie I told to reassure someone. The first in a long series leading up to today. I remember realizing that her fears were allayed when I told her what she wanted to hear. Meanwhile, it was just the opposite: nothing tempted me more than this prohibition. I dreamed of the tracks and the train. About getting as near to it as I could. Counting the cars from up close. At last. I imagined the noises. I invented emotions. I needed to experience it.

My friends and I envisioned repeating the scene in *Lucky Luke*: putting an ear to the rail and hearing the train coming in the distance. Anticipating it. Hearing its vibrations, like hearing the ocean's waves vibrating in the big seashell that had been sitting for as long as I can remember on my grandmother's toilet tank. It was pink, pearlescent on the inside. I also remember my disenchantment when I understood, years later, that it wasn't the ocean that you heard but the amplified echo of ambient vibrations. The truth is so disappointing. Which is why, I believe, that I became an artist.

The train was something authentic. I had understood that I could finally get close to reality. Luc had told us that when you put a nickel on the track, the train squashed it to the size of a quarter and that apparently "it works in the arcade machines at the arena." We believed him because of his older brother. From that moment on, I collected all the five-cent pieces I could find. I traded dimes and pennies for nickels at the convenience store. The clerk did not understand why.

I had tried to flatten a coin, using a hammer and anvil, but to no avail. The hammer rebounded and I felt the vibrations in my forearm for two days.

It was becoming increasingly clear that this would require the train.

The bicycle gave me my first taste of real freedom. As significant as the lies. First, because the bike moved me faster than running did, but especially because the feeling of the wind had seemed like the most wonderful of all caresses. I went fast. Faster than walking. Faster than all the girls, too, who couldn't have cared less about this hidden aspect of boys. Well, almost all of them. There was one, Arielle, a redhead with freckles, especially in summer, who was kind of a tomboy and who could have been one of my friends. At that age, boys don't have girls as friends. It would be like a betrayal of gender. By both parties.

Arielle and I kept our distance from each other, despite the attraction. As you do with the abyss when you're high above it.

I had gotten very good at avoiding her. During school hours, I knew at any given moment where she was in the building and who she was talking to. Knowing your enemy's location gives you an advantage. Only a few years later, she confessed that she'd been doing the same thing. And the more we kept our distance, the more the attraction grew.

I wanted so badly for her to come play with us on the tracks that summer. I pictured myself explaining to her where to go and how far from the train to stand for it to be just scary enough but no risk to our lives. I didn't want to frighten her. Or only a little. Just enough, so that she'd admire me. But I kept all that a secret. The one time I'd told the boys that she wanted to join us, after school one Friday in June, I'd been subjected to a hail of protests:

"What's her problem? Doesn't she have any friends?"

"Are you crazy, Marc? Not Arielle, she's gonna slow us down."

"Why her? The other girls are going to follow her... then they'll rat us out, for sure."

I had swallowed my words, acting as if it were the worst idea in the world. Even if it had been mine to begin with. In a move confirming that we had good reason to steer clear of girls. It was also one of the first inconsistencies in my short life: a feeling impossible to honour. And one that I had to hide from my gang.

The only time the two of us ever walked along the railroad tracks, years later, I told her about that memory.

It was also the first time I'd intended to kill her. But I would never tell her so. I've always carried a burden of hate equal to the love I bear. No idea why.

Summer gradually approached. School would soon be over. Vacation, at last. Whole days of freedom. With my friends. We had a million projects and a million more plans. One day, we'd go to the sandpit. We'd also go up on the trestle. An iron suspension bridge woven like lace. We'd build a cabin out of hemlock branches. We'd blow up model cars with firecrackers. We'd also blow up frogs and toads with some of those same firecrackers. We'd spy on the girls, from a distance. We'd swim, too. Luc, Samuel, George and me.

Luc had no schedule. He was the friend my mother did not like. He had no set schedule; his parents worked all the time. His older brother, who was 15, took care of him. My other friend, Samuel, had two sisters. One was younger and insignificant in our eyes, and one was older – 14. We spied on her when she went swimming. We were always game to go swimming when his sister was there. Everything our avid eyes could snatch was worth its weight in gold. She wore a one-piece Speedo with blue and white stripes. I could draw her with my eyes closed. I imagined her breasts through her swimsuit. The cold water made them stand out against the fabric. When her back was turned, my eyes roamed over her ass.

And George, the other friend. His real name was George Ahmed Mougharbel. Lebanese, Muslim. We called him George at school. The first time we went to his house, we learned that our George was actually Ahmed. That's what his parents called him. "George" was to help him fit in here.

His father was a chemical engineer and a geologist for the Department of Natural Resources. First generation immigrants. The Mougharbel family had left a war-torn Lebanon. A suburb of Beirut, with enough bombs to scare you. And just enough money to dream of living elsewhere. Everyone in his family was talented. His mother, Ahha, taught mathematics at the university. His sisters, who were older than us, were sweet and very polite. We were impressed by their impeccable French accent. French, as in France. I always admired people who give up everything to make a new life somewhere else. It takes pluck and courage, sometimes some fear as well, to leave behind everything you knew about yourself.

Sometimes, when you transplant flowers, a number of them refuse the uprooting. Often, the new soil has a different pH and they don't take. There are some very simple rules. Arielle's the one who told me that. Years later.

That summer, we four friends were together from morning till night. Seven days a week. Except for the family-vacation weeks, which we all separately but unanimously considered to be too long and essentially useless because they were staggered.

Although I ran into Arielle from time to time, particularly since I delivered the newspaper to her house, I had managed fairly well to keep her out of our boys' life. Even if I did have the slightly unhappy feeling about deceiving her. To our unspoken satisfaction, we boys had never discussed it again during those 10 weeks of vacation.

George-Ahmed was different from us. It was obvious. He didn't eat the same things. His house smelled of something else: spices unfamiliar to us. And his whole family was religious. Much more so than we were. Prayer was sacred.

We didn't know it yet but our parents – the middle class – had stopped being observant and had abandoned their religion. A rupture. Ahmed's family seemed to revolve around a focal point that we were missing. And then there was television. They did not watch it. Like my mother. Yet for us kids, and all the other grown-ups I knew, it was an essential barrier. A form of passive identity. Perfect for my autism. I could watch the same movie dozens of times.

Other than *The Littlest Hobo*, with the crime-solving dog, nothing we saw on television resonated with George-Ahmed. So we played. We created worlds out of nothing. With a knife, actually a pocketknife, we rebuilt the world with branches, ropes and rocks. We told each other tons of stories. That summer, I discovered that when my friends showed an interest, I was able to invent a reality that could enchant. One that they believed in. They trusted me. This was new, a power that I was discovering. I knew how to tell a story.

One deathly hot and humid Sunday in July, Sam got a flat tire by riding over the big stones on the road to the sand quarry. We had taken our chances going there, outside of operating hours.

We all went back to Sam's house, walking next to our bikes in solidarity. We set ourselves up in his garage to become mechanics, just for an afternoon. It was cooler there than in the sun. While Luc, Sam and I were convinced that we could repair the split tire with electrical tape, Ahmed said, "Don't do that. I'll be back in ten minutes. Marc, come with me."

"Okay."

We biked like mad to his house, standing up on our pedals the whole way. Proud. Thrilled to be doing something. Because he'd chosen me to go with him, he and I bonded even more. A form of respect. Even as children. He had chosen me. At that precise moment, Med became my best friend.

He rummaged through the shed behind his house for a few minutes and muttered words, surely happily, in Arabic, showing me something in his hand and smiling victoriously.

As we got back on our bikes, I met the eyes of one of his sisters. I thought she was beautiful. Dark eyes, worried but lovely. I froze. She stared at me. Ahmed yelled something. To him, it was just his sister. I remember standing stock-still because he had to tell me, still shouting, with an accent halfway between his own and a Quebecker's, "Come *on*, Marc!" He rolled the 'r' in my name. And then to his sister Rima: "Leave him alone already. He's a friend mine."

I also saw his father's silhouette through the patio door. The same silhouette I'd see at Ahmed's funeral, a few weeks later.

Med had remembered and found his father's emergency puncture repair kit. We went back to join Sam and Luc in the garage. We followed the directions very carefully, all reading at the same time. In the end, I was the one Med asked to handle the instruction sheet: scratch the surface with the little metal file, cut out a piece of rubber, apply the glue to the inner surface of the tire and the piece of rubber… That hot and humid afternoon in the summer of 1981, in the shade of a suburban garage, we repaired Sam's flat tire with all the gravitas in the world, convinced that we were accomplishing something extraordinary.

The next day, because we'd had to wait 24 hours, we pumped up the tire and it held. I remember feeling invincible; everything was possible. I had no idea why Med, as we now called Ahmed, knew how to repair a bicycle tire. Probably something about his culture, I thought. Where I came from, foreign places and foreign people had more information than we did. He was way ahead of us. He'd been right.

That evening, which happened to be a Monday, I listened to Pierre Pascau on *L'Informateur en rappel*. Every evening on CKAC, I lay in bed and listened as this public affairs broadcast summarized the day. On a radio-alarm clock with a sleep function that waited one hour before automatically shutting itself off. A device from RadioShack's Realistic line, which I'd bought with money from my paper route. I remember that on that July evening, there was a report about the unsolved murder of a woman in Pointe-aux-Trembles. Everyone on the radio agreed on the identity of the killer, who was never convicted due to a lack of evidence or to procedural errors, I don't remember which. I fell asleep to the voice of the radio host who, infuriated by the judicial system, was complaining like all get-out, impotent but with a voice that echoed both the prevailing social "injustice" and the people calling in to complain about criminal proceedings.

Arielle, however, didn't seem to be concerned by my exile to the world of boys. I was wrong about that. She would later tell me how excluded she'd felt by our indifference.

It was also through her that I learned the importance of keeping up appearances and portraying emotions. Its usefulness. For tricking people's minds.

"Like I didn't exist anymore, Marc…"

Far from considering, let alone *feeling*, her distress, I spent the first few weeks of summer vacation with my friends, enjoying a simple, easy happiness. Getting up, eating two pieces of bread with peanut butter and Nutella. Sometimes adding round slices of banana.

The only dramas we experienced were the ones we invented for ourselves. Often recklessly. Like the bicycle courses we set up. Luc had a BMX mountain bike. I had a stopwatch, also purchased with money from my paper route. A watch that gave me an advantage over my friends. It was new, and a rarity, with digital numbers. A far cry from the hands on a standard dial. My friends were fascinated by the technology, whereas I was fascinated by time. My only ally. As it still is today. The clock-radio wasn't enough. I set two alarms in the morning. Triumphant.

Later in life, I developed a hatred for the radio and an even greater hatred for the kind of adults who listen to it to camouflage their fear of silence and occupy their minds. But during my childhood, the radio filled a portion of my hours.

On weekend evenings, when the broadcasts were boring, I played a time game: I tried to count off the seconds at the same pace as the timer on my watch, without looking. When I got to 30 or 60 in my head, I checked to see how many seconds had passed. At first, when I got it exactly right, it had something to do with luck. By the end of the summer, I had gotten good at it. I always did have a talent for simultaneity. Even more so for synchronicity, even if I didn't know what the word meant when I was 11. I was off to a good start.

This was a fact. I was born under a lucky star and life would offer me a million coincidences. I've always been blessed with good instincts. Between appropriate silences and the right words, I almost always manage to be authentic. The world likes people who are authentic.

Summer days passed with the same rules and the same schedule. My mother, who worked as a research assistant in biology at Concordia University, insisted that I be home every day at noon. She called, to check. Every evening, she told me what she'd made for lunch the following day. I wore a key around my neck on a piece of red wool, which made me crazy because the yarn prickled my skin. Like most of the clothes she bought for me.

I hid the key in the peonies every time I went out. I pretty much raised myself. With the silence of a house, sometimes the sound of a radio in the evening, lots of books, and

Tupperware containers holding white-bread sandwiches with baked ham or a slice of Kraft cheese, still in its wrapper so the bread wouldn't get soggy. Sometimes I had carrots or celery. With Vachon caramel or Jos Louis cakes, and a tasteless apple, for dessert.

Thanks to my Casio watch and its alarm, a revolutionary addition to my life, I knew exactly how many minutes I was from home. To appease my mother. No matter where I was, my watch buzzed at 11:50 a.m. I jumped on my bike and pedalled either quickly or at a normal pace, depending on the urgency. I was always at home at exactly 12:05 p.m. That's when she called.

"Yes, Mom; no, Mom. I went to Sam's, we played in the woods behind his house, we went to the pond; no, Mom, yes, I ate. No, we didn't listen to the fight on TV; yes, the celery and carrots, and the apple; yes, I brought in the mail… Me too, see you tonight."

At 11, I knew that one of my responsibilities was to reassure my mother. I had learned to gain her trust. Midway between lies and good intentions. Which, according to my calculations, was a weight I was able to bear. Along with the guilt that came with it. I knew how to handle it.

Everything in the future would be better. I learned that summer that the ability to keep others – adults – calm would be essential to my survival. Especially police officers and psychologists. Later, this would include women, and Arielle.

We spent rainy days on Luc's veranda. He had a Tyco miniature electric train on a plywood table covered with fake grass. Little bridges, tunnels, resin lakes, tiny humans and railroad crossings. We played a bit, but it was already an old game. It was there, on the miniature model, that we planned our trick of making 25¢ pieces on the tracks, which we would perform a few days later.

We talked a lot about the arcade games at the arena. They were a novelty. The first video games. There was Donkey Kong, Space Invaders, Asteroids, and Pac-Man. But money was hard to come by, especially quarters.

It was a stormy afternoon, and if something has to take the blame it might as well be the lightning. We officially decided that the train was going to help us convert nickels into quarters. Going to play video games was sort of forbidden by our families. They were new and mysterious. Playing at the arena, in the middle of summer, was frowned upon. As if we were wasting our time. Loitering. And video games came from somewhere else, from far away. They were scary.

The skating rink was open on a reduced schedule but the Elite hockey leagues' summer camps were held there. We were fascinated by the tons of snow that the Zamboni piled up outside despite the 30° Celsius temperatures. I played there three days a week, every week, even in the summertime.

That was the only rationale I could offer my mother for going to the arena: I was good at hockey and played PeeWee AA during the rest of the year. Elite League. It would be normal for me to hang around the municipal arena for part of the summer. I transported my equipment bag in the newspaper cart attached to the back of my bicycle. I made it to every practice and game. It was a pretext that, at the very least, my friends' parents considered to be valid, and so the boys were able to come meet me after games and training sessions.

Sam was the first one to suggest putting coins on the railroad tracks. I remember the silent fractions of seconds after he spoke. No one wanted to be a chicken, so we agreed to go together the next day. A pact.

That night, in my bed, two new feelings arose: euphoria and guilt. Together. They are connected all too often.

My little 11-year-old brain began to make plans to avoid getting caught. Two of us would keep watch while the other two would go put the coins on the rail. Without looking like we were up to something. That was the main thing: to avoid arousing suspicion.

The rendezvous was set for the next day at my house, where we would prepare our stunt. We would do it with the evening train. Everyone came with his own plan but mine was the one we settled on. I think it was my calm demeanour that convinced them. I'd known for a long time, because of my reading, that people who do not hesitate are one step ahead of the curve. People tend to believe them.

At the end of the day, we were feverishly excited as we hitched my newspaper delivery cart to my bike to create a diversion and to go unnoticed. We pedalled along Des Sœurs to the railroad crossing. I had filled the cart with brown-paper grocery bags, which I'd then stuffed with even more bags and old newspapers. We thought this would make it look like we were actually doing something. It would look legitimate.

It's hesitations that betray us. I already knew it at the age of 11.

As we left my garage, the bags, which were too light, fell to the ground. We stopped to collect stones along the side of the road to add weight and stabilize the load. I remember the dandelions and the wild daisies growing in between the rocks along the shoulder. And a blue flower, small and very pretty. That calmed me down. As far back as I can remember, I've always loved flowers. They've been a great help.

"Hey, let's get a move on," Sam said to Ahmed and me.

"Go help them!" Luc yelled from far ahead of us.

"Shut yer trap!"

"Hey, we're doing our best! We're coming."

"Speed it up, or we're gonna to miss the train!"

We got there in time. Luc and Sam pretended to be playing together alongside the ditch beside the road near the tracks while Med and I took the trail through the woods that bordered the railroad. They stayed there until we'd placed the nickels on the rail.

"I think it's coming."

"No, Med, it was just a truck. Take your time and put them down the way you're supposed to."

The air smelled of the creosote in the treated wood. We could be seen from the road. The plan was for Luc and Sam to attract the attention of cars on their side of the road while Med and I took care of business. I imagined the concern of drivers seeing kids playing by the tracks. And the impression this could make on memories. To avoid raising suspicion, you have to be average. Ordinary folks never go onto railway tracks.

Once our job was done, Med and I took shelter a few metres away, in a little woodlot bordering the rails.

"Don't move. *Do not move.* What they see is movement," I said. "We stay still."

"Okay."

Med had impressed me. He had nerves of steel; he stayed calm. I had good reason to respect him. He was definitely my friend. Dependable.

We waited 4 minutes and 48 seconds. The train arrived precisely at its scheduled time. At 5:02 p.m., as usual. First, we felt the ground vibrating. A few seconds later, train sounds: metal rubbing against metal, hydraulic noises, and air compression, along with the sounds of stones clattering between the railroad ties. Then the bells sounding at the crossing. *Ding-ding-ding-ding-ding-ding.* Much louder than I had imagined. I thought about my mother. I would have smiled, had I been able to.

The first locomotive appeared before us. Gigantic and slow. A few coins had fallen off the rail before the train could run over them. Due to the vibrations. But several had stayed in place, at least for a few cars. We were ecstatic. We felt very much alive.

When the lead locomotive – and there were three – arrived at the crossing, the train blew its whistle. That's when I smiled. Luc and Sam waved their arms at the conductor, signaling him to pull on the whistle's cord. Just like in the movies. Every little boy in the world dreams of one day having a train whistle for him. The conductor would be content with this simple, happy reality without looking back in our direction.

From our outpost, we counted the train's cars. Med counted 79, and I counted 78. The evening train never had a caboose. The last freight car passed before us. Even slower than the head of the train, it seemed, because we had discussed it at the time. From our hideout, we could see the crossing, but as soon as the head of the train went through it, the tracks veered to the right, and the conductor could no longer see us. We were standing up, ready to pounce.

"The front part goes faster because of the locomotives," I'd said with confidence. But I was not certain of what I was claiming. Just convinced of it. To this day, I still believe it but still don't know why the head of a train seems to go faster than the tail.

Then all was quiet again. We rushed to the rails as soon as the bells stopped ringing, as if it were a signal. I remember the first coin I picked up: it was blazing hot, heated by friction. Flattened. Uneven but as big as a 25¢ piece. Med and I were jubilant. We picked up all the coins and went to join our friends.

That night, the last time I checked the clock, it was 1:22 a.m.

First thing the next morning, in Luc's garage, we used a hammer to round off the deformed, uneven edges of the coins and then we made them match as closely as possible the diameter of a quarter, using a real coin as a template.

A train, a vise and a hammer. At 11 a.m., the arena doors would open. The snack bar already reeked of French fries, rancid oil, and vinegar. Toward the back, the lights flashed on the arcade games, which were making electronic noises. All of it beckoned. We played 13 rounds. Sixty-five cents instead of $3.25. Life was beautiful. To us. Sheer joy.

In one fell swoop, our horizons were broadened. We'd had an idea and it had worked out perfectly. A miracle. For once, we had an impact on our desires, aside from biking and catching frogs in dead, green ponds. Our recent accomplishment brought us out of childhood.

We did it again three days later. This time, Sam came with me to put the coins on the rail while Luc and Med stood guard by the road. Sam and Med fussed a little, wanting to know why we were changing an arrangement that had already worked once. Med objected the most. Because in the hierarchy of tasks, ours were the more valuable. We knew it but kept quiet. We did, however, share equally. I don't know why no one wanted to take my place. As if I were indisputably indispensable in my role. This feeling was always part of my life. Being in charge. As many desires as feelings, especially the ones I didn't have. An identity. My own. Circumstances would inevitably teach me that this was only natural.

The second time, as I was delivering my newspapers in the afternoon, I saw Arielle near her house. She was walking her dog. She always walked him at the same time every day. This I knew.

I first felt and then met her gaze, which was penetrating. I was convinced that she had figured things out. Yet she and I had chosen to avoid each other since the end of the school year.

That Monday in July, she looked me straight in the eye for several seconds, and a burden of guilt surged through me. I was on the verge of telling her everything, but I resisted. Choked back the confession. To this day, I remain convinced that she suspected. Despite the triumphant attitude I thought I was projecting. Acting as if nothing was going on. At 11, I already knew that other people's perceptions of me, even if they were correct, did not exist unless they were acknowledged. And I thought that if I managed to make a whole bunch of 25¢ pieces and got really good at Donkey Kong, maybe she would think highly of me come September. At night in bed, I pictured a video game tournament organized by the school, and all the students were in the gym where I won the contest, and I looked at her and she thought I was handsome.

I held her long look only a fraction of a second longer than usual. A speck of time. An infinite amount of meaning.

We ended the look just in time. Fortunately. Beautiful Arielle. It was thanks to her that I could lie to the authorities was such aplomb a few weeks later. Yet once again, I am certain, she had figured everything out. And decided to cover for me. I clung desperately to this idea in the months that followed. To go on. Only the two of us knew.

So that Monday, after I'd delivered my papers, we repeated our caper, this time doubling the number of nickels. Laid on both rails. There were the four of us. Sam looked at me with a big smile, once the train had passed and rolled out of sight.

"Easy," he'd said.

He was right. Once the locomotive went through the crossing, a final whistle blew. We had moved closer to the track to have a better vantage point. The railway cars passed slowly before us, making their metallic racket. Luc had said it was like in the mountains of Russia. The ground moved and vibrated. We were at least a metre from the train's wheels. I could have touched them. There were no more boundaries.

The government-mandated construction holiday came in mid-July. It would separate us for two weeks. Sam was going to spend the first week at summer camp and the second in Maine. Luc and his uncle were spending the second week at Canada's Wonderland. We were down to three. It wasn't the same. For me either because it was the only time of the year, aside from the week of Christmas, when I didn't have hockey. The only break. My mother had always thought that the best way to keep her son on the right track and to make something of him was to keep him busy. Through discipline. An idea that came from her father.

I played hockey and I was very good, a natural talent. With a little work, I could have been better.

When you're a member of an Elite league, you get special treatment. A driver was available to take me to all the practices, but I preferred to go by myself, on my bike. Keeping my distance.

On game days, the coach insisted that we all go together. In a chartered bus, if we were playing in another town. We learned to say "Sir" and to be polite. On game days, we had to wear a shirt and tie to the arena. Codes of behaviour that I respected. I understood.

My mother's vacation always came at the end of August. During that dead period when the run-up to the new school year becomes intolerable. When the tourists have all gone home. A bit off-season, but still during the summer. Med and his family never seemed to take a vacation. I thought that maybe they didn't need one. Sometimes, in the evening, I pondered all the determination it would take to start life over, in a new place. To go in a different direction. To have the strength to divert destiny, especially Med's. To switch from one track to another.

By the end of July, we missed Sam. For the entire week, we stayed away from the train tracks and the arena. We had a clan mentality. Solidarity. Our sense of honour seemed rock solid. Until Luc also went away. Med and I felt as if we had to wait a long time for them to come back. And it seemed even longer when we pictured them somewhere, having fun without us. In the shared world that we maintained, everything went on as usual.

One day my mother noticed that whenever I set the table, I always aligned the utensils with the clock on the wall. I was eight years old. I'd already been lining up all kinds of things for quite some time, like chips in order of size before eating them. She simply remarked on the fact without forcing the issue. A little bit concerned but nothing more. I did well in school and I was courteous. Enough to slip under the radar.

When she spoke to me, I noticeably moved my head so that her right ear lobe, which I kept staring at, was in line with some object I'd spotted in the near distance: a lamp, a photograph, a chair. When I lay in bed at night, all my stuffed toys had to be in an order that I had devised one day. The bedding too. The contour sheet, the cotton sheet, then the quilt, all untouched. I slept on top of my perfectly made bed. On the bedspread, under two fleece blankets. The first worn and soft as satin. The second, newer, with a pattern of dogs' heads. For several years, I slept in my clothes. My toothbrush had to be red. I only fell asleep with a sweater over my eyes, like a wolf. But it was the weight of the garment that soothed me. The same for my toy lion, stuffed with beans, the heaviest, resting on my chest.

I always secured the shadows, made by the street's lamp-post shining through the silver maple in front of the house, to a three-masted sailboat wallpapered onto one of the walls of my room. If I didn't, I had trouble falling asleep. And every Monday, I had to wear my Bugs Bunny underwear. Otherwise, disaster or some kind of misfortune. I didn't feel well. I was discombobulated. The same thing with clothes: I could not wear anything but well-worn cotton. All other fabrics irritated my skin.

I managed to keep it all inside, to hide everything from my mother. For her own good. Obviously. So I wouldn't worry her. She had her hands full with her schedule, the house to keep up, my hockey all year long, and her vast sense of mother's guilt.

Med and I continued to spend our days the way kids do. We built a cabin-cave out of hemlock branches without removing their needles. It smelled good.

We hunted frogs in the ponds with a stick, a fishing line, a hook and a scrap of red fabric. The frogs were curious about red. Intrigued, they'd approach the bit of cloth and just as they'd pass near or on top, ha! We'd strike and the hook would snag them. I remember one time we caught an enormous bullfrog, and when we took it out of the water, it unhooked itself. Med had yelled at me, as if we were losing a treasure.

"Marc, quick, it's gonna get away!"

I jumped up, and the only thing that came to mind was to put my foot on it. I squashed it. Not good for anything anymore. Even our garter snakes wouldn't want it. They ate only live frogs. Grasshoppers and crickets, too.

In early spring, garter snakes leave their winter hideaways and warm themselves in the sun. We laid out sheets of tin roofing in the middle of a field, and in the first hours of daylight, the snakes would curl up on them for warmth. Our vivarium was a wooden box made of four-by-four-foot particleboards that were three feet high. We added some branches, peat, grass, humus, rocks, and each week, a few frogs. We were fascinated. The snake took hours to swallow a frog, which was three or four times bigger than its mouth. The snake dislocated its jaw to gently swallow its meal in silence. It had a huge bump in its body for the few days it took to digest its food. It was ugly and beautiful at the same time. The frog didn't die instantly; it moved a long time after having been devoured. I was spellbound.

We liked Med a lot because he was the one who caught the snakes. By the tail. He wasn't afraid of being bitten. "It's nothing," he said. We lifted the roofing sheets one by one and yelled, "Med, quick, it's getting away. Here, here, here…*yesssss!*"

Med held onto it and everyone talked at once. The snake wriggled and swung at the end of his arm. We walked our bicycles back home in triumph. All the children from neighbouring streets came to meet us. To see what they would never do themselves. We didn't have any real reason to capture snakes, other than to scare girls. All the girls were afraid, except Arielle, who said they didn't bother her. That may partially explain why I thought I was in love with her.

Arielle was different.

She never wanted to hold one in her hand but she came close enough to our "snake-pit" for me to believe her. She watched the reptiles eat the frogs with as much wonderment as I did. She stayed there and did not look away. We brushed up against each other. Side by side. Witnessing the same pragmatic, cruel beauty. We told each other that we wouldn't want to die that way.

"Look at his tongue coming out like a snake's." She was right.

Every evening, my mother made me swear that our snakes couldn't escape from their box. She would have fainted dead away if she'd found a snake in the house. I was happy that Arielle didn't share her fear. I got the impression that Arielle was strong and that I could tell her my secrets. Connections are sometimes woven far from intentions. I knew I could trust her even before I needed her. Arielle, with her precise details, proved to be invaluable when the police asked her about me. Today, I know that my 11th year went on as expected, largely thanks to her.

July 31, 1981.

A Friday. The whole day was hot and sticky. The crickets sang in broad daylight. My mother had washed my hockey equipment. It was drying on the clothesline. I missed hockey and couldn't wait to start playing again.

My mother's birthday was July 31, which makes her a Leo. It was also the first time during the summer, as it was every year, that corn was available at the farmers' markets.

As I recall, every July 31 we ate roast corn and nothing else. In 1981, the Indian corn was yellow. That night, we again ate corn. A reassuring ritual. I did the husking. I loved the sound the leaves made as I tore them.

Since morning, the day had unfolded uneventfully. Med and I were alone and had gone out to ride our bikes. We made it to the Gauvin Quarry sandpit just before noon. It was full of fine sand. As long we stayed on the groomed trails, everything was okay. As soon as we went off them, we had to pedal twice as hard to get through the shifting sand. In the soft, loose sand, we sank and came to a halt. We had to get off our bikes if we wanted to go any further. It was infuriating to have our ride interrupted. Seen as a failure. I blamed myself for not being able to keep going. For not being strong enough. I hate it when things don't go as planned.

Once back on a road packed down by the trucks, we felt reborn. Free again.

As far back as I can remember, I always resented being slowed down by things beyond my control. It made me uncomfortable.

At the very bottom of the quarry, there was a lake. Carved out by men, dynamite, and machines, and filled by spring water and rain. A dark, cavernous blue. We assumed that it was deep and fantasized about swimming or fishing in it. We imagined it was home to sea monsters. A body of water that dreams are made of. One day, we would see the lakebed. Med and I threw tons of pebbles into it on that morning of July 31. We could spend ages searching through the sand and gravel for flat rocks. Flat rocks to skip across the water.

Sometimes, nine or 10 bounces in a row, on the surface. We counted carefully, especially the ones at the end, which were closer together. And unequivocal when it came to choosing a winner, even if we were true friends.

We also had contests to see who could throw the furthest and Med always won. He had a better arm than I did. I remember his arms. They were muscular for a boy our age. It was probably because of the lawns he mowed during the summer. A job that required strength. When we went our separate ways at the end of the day, it was often so that Med could fulfil his mowing contracts and I could deliver my papers.

I also recall a big stone that Med once threw. I heard the sound of the water and watched the little waves for a long time. I was always fascinated by the concentric circles that gradually moved further from the point of impact and finally disappeared. Today, I know that this is like our memories.

"She's not so bad, eh, that Arielle?"

It took me a few seconds to realize what he had just said. Stunned. Unable to utter a sound. Acting cool. Not reacting. Not giving anything away. Pretending it was a trivial matter.

Then he added, "What do you think of her?"

"She's okay, she's a girl. Yeah, she's all right. But she's still a girl."

Arielle and I had almost danced together at a class party at the end of the school year. It was all in the cards. It was the two of us, we knew it. But we hadn't been able to show it in front of everyone. We would have been the first and that made it too intimidating. Everybody knew and felt our connection. Invisible, or so we believed. Everything was so palpable. Attractions – real ones – are like trains.

Why had Med talked to me about her? I thought it was to make me admit it. Men have this direct way of coming out of nowhere and questioning each other; it's like a confrontation. I thought he did it to make me tell him about Arielle. To make me spell it out for him. But he should have known. It was impossible that he didn't.

"Because I'm going to ask her to be my girlfriend this year," Med said. He was serious. I knew what he meant. Med was dependable.

Express my fury or supress it. Let him know that she was mine, incriminate myself, or stay quiet and keep pretending in order to stay strong. I decided to keep my mouth shut.

In actual fact, to hide this sudden craving for violence, I immediately and contemptuously wished him "Good luck." As if she were nothing to me. But at that very moment, my friend became someone else. We went home, each to his own house, at noon.

Then just before we separated, I said, "Med, are we going to the train tonight to make 25¢ pieces, for Luc and Sam, before they come back?"

Whatever it took to change the mood. I needed to heighten my existence, to feel a little more alive than usual because Arielle was mine and Med was my friend. Trying to forget what had just transpired.

This need to exist took up all the space. We would go flatten coins. Because it was forbidden. And because it got the blood going. The blood accelerating in our veins, justifying our actions.

Taking it up a notch. We agreed. Based on the desire to amaze our absent friends. On Monday, when they returned, we'd be heroes. They'd know how brave we were. Med and I hadn't gone on vacation but we'd have forged ahead. We would be courageous. There are always moments that make more of a lasting impression. Although we don't know why, they define us more than anything else. Even when only casually mentioned projects or ideas are involved.

We planned to meet after lunch. At that point, we'd decide what to do next. Med also had three lawns to mow. Friday was his busiest day.

"Med, don't show up late. Because today is my mom's birthday."

"No, I'll meet you here, I promise."

On this count, he was unfailing. Always kept his word. You could trust him. Precisely my concern.

I told myself that Med would never come.

I spent the rest of the afternoon alone. Watching TV. A Disney movie. *Race to Witch Mountain*. A story about twins with incredible magic powers. I'd already seen the movie several times. I knew it by heart.

Around 3:00 p.m., I prepared my bike and the cart I attached behind it. The newspapers had just been delivered to my house. At 3:20 p.m., I left to make my rounds.

At 4:30, I ran into Arielle, at her house. We chatted for 10 whole minutes. Until 4:40. Our longest conversation since classes had ended. I was so happy. She asked how my summer was going and for news of my friends. "Seems like you four are always together."

"Yeah, we get along great."

I would have loved to tell her more about them. About them because of her. About her, the one I pinned my hopes on. But my age prevented me from having the strength to do it.

I did, however, tell her about the tracks and how we played there. I told her what we did on them and how it worked. I wanted to impress her, make her see that we were really brave. I so badly wanted her to admire me. To exist in her eyes. To make her think I was special.

I had always thought that girls liked boys who were kind of rebellious. Like in the movies. Especially the boys who didn't show it. I was very careful not to have emotions or to invent them. So that she'd feel I wasn't afraid. I was sure of it.

What followed proved me right: she and I would make it past the simple day-to-day of that summer of our 11th year. We'd become adults together. Lead lives that were parallel and linked. Railroad tracks.

I felt the nickels' weight in my left pocket.

"Okay, I'm gonna go, the train's coming soon."

We said things to each other, in those 10 minutes. Some of them were inconsequential. And others, suffused with things to come.

Arielle and I, I now know, had yearned for each other. The words hadn't been spoken; they'd been promised in silence. I knew it. Ten minutes on one summer day. There are things that need no explanation.

Ten minutes that were going to change my life.

"Bye, Arielle."

"Bye, Marc."

I left her house around 4:40 p.m. The time it took me to get home. It was 4:45 p.m.

My mother came home from work every afternoon around 5:20 p.m. I'd make it in time for her birthday dinner. The train passed every evening from 5:02 p.m. to 5:03 p.m. A metronome. Once, on April 19, even from afar, I checked the time by looking at my watch and it had whistled at 5:04. I remembered all the trains, their early and late arrivals. Don't know why, nor do I know why I always think of Arielle at 11:11 a.m. For years, and still to this day, I set the alarms on my watch and telephone to go off that time. Every single day. To think of her.

My mother was happy to eat Indian corn for dinner on July 31. I hurriedly made her a bouquet with the wild flowers I'd gathered beside the railway tracks and a few others I'd stolen from a neighbour: phlox, asters, iris, gentian, pimpernel. I liked it a lot when she was smiling and carefree. I felt responsible. My mother was strong. She raised me by herself, my father having left to start a new life in Illinois with another woman when I was five years old. She was my family, along with her parents – my grandparents, who were also at dinner that night – her two sisters and their husbands. Three cousins, one boy and two girls.

Everyone admired her, especially the women in the family, for being alone with a child. I was her little man. She would make a grown man of me.

Often, part of the burden of being responsible for our own happiness comes from others and from their expectations. But everything was easy with my mom. We were happy together, just the two of us. Although she cried a fair amount, more often than I did, in any case. If we're keeping score, her smiles outweighed the hardships. I think. I know that she sometimes cried at night, alone.

Hence it was important that I stay with her.

I went to bed as usual that night. No moaning and groaning. In fact, I let my mother tell me when it was bedtime so that she would feel useful. The time I spent in bed each night, alone with the radio and my thoughts, was often the greatest pleasure of my day. Because at any moment, I could shut off the radio broadcaster's voice if it became too intrusive.

It was then that I invented worlds on the walls and the ceiling. Stretched out end to end, the hours passed staring at the ceiling would add up to months.

I also did a lot of calculations in my head. As many mathematical as situational. I would imagine questions that I might ask of people I'd see the next day and try to predict their answers. Secretly, these were small victories. I found it comforting to have a schedule and to know what the next day would bring. I pictured the people I would meet. Like a game of chess. I got very good at guessing their identities and postulating events.

I spent hours anticipating everything I might be asked. With a thousand potential responses. Like a computer language. Nothing missing. Nothing and no one would gain the upper hand. A race against time and the world.

I had a sense of existing endlessly when I managed to get a jump on the present. A present too banal for me. I know that now. Living a simple life would not be enough. I'd need more.

At 9:19 p.m., the telephone rang. Distant sounds. My mother's voice, which I could hear through the walls. Two minutes later, she was in my room.

"Marc, Med didn't come home tonight. Any idea where he might be?"

"No, we played together at the pit this morning… I came home to eat, you and I talked, he was supposed to come meet me after lunch but he didn't show up so I watched a movie."

I was a little worried. Nervous at having admitted to her that we'd been at the pit. She did not want me to go to that place. My mother confused the dread she heard in my voice when I made this confession with Med's absence because she tried to be reassuring when she came and sat on my bed and ran her fingers through my hair. She was happy when she thought she was making me happy.

"Not to worry. I'm sure he'll be home soon, but his father's concerned."

The evening of July 31 was a beautiful one. A warm, starry summer night with a glow in the west, even at 9:30. Everything might have been normal.

"G'night, Mom. Happy birthday, I love you."

"Thanks, darling. Sweet dreams."

"Yeah, I'm gonna try to dream about you."

It made her laugh when I told her that. Touched first by the words themselves, and then by the hidden meaning; I told her the same thing every night. In the darkness, she pictured me smiling.

"Turn off your radio and go to sleep."

"Love you, too."

The sun had been up for a few hours when a knock on the front door woke me up. A neighbour lady. It was 7:03 a.m. according to both my watch and my alarm clock. It matters to me that the time be correct everywhere.

My mother had gone to answer the door. I heard her speaking.

"Yes, he's here. In his room. He's sleeping."

The morning train had come to a halt and was blocking the level crossing. Police cars all over the place. An ambulance. A white truck. A fire engine. Several men standing about, also appearing not to move. I could see them off in the distance, all the way from my house. From time to time, one of them walked. Another one, further back and to the left, was covered from head to toe by a white jumpsuit. I was on the lawn.

Motionless. Inoperative, like the train. My mother was stern and nervous. I felt it. Then, holding me more tightly against her than usual, she told me what the neighbour had told her.

Med's body was found in four pieces. Cut through the middle of his stomach. The forearms, with the legs severed at the pelvis, outside the railroad tracks. The torso with the head and the arms up to the elbows, in between the two rails. The morning train had been unable to stop in time. The conductor told the policemen that the body had already been dismembered when he rolled over it. Too late to stop.

There were crows too, on the ground. It was actually the crows that he'd seen before anything else. Birds are unsentimental when it comes to their survival. They ate. The conductor had seen one mass, then another. A body, he thought. With the sole consolation that it wasn't his train that had run Med over. It wasn't his fault. Med was already dead.

I did not go look. I did not go near, despite the allure. What I was told over the days and weeks and months that followed was enough for me to envision the scene. I preferred to lie on my bed and stare at the ceiling some more. Connecting, through the emptiness, the death of my friend to my life.

I remained in silence until noon. My mother came to see me, plagued by worry and disbelief. To find out how I was. Asking me if I had something to say, if I wanted to talk or if I was hungry. She insisted that I talk.

"No, Mom, I'm fine, but it's really weird, like it isn't really real. Like I'm going to wake up."

"I know, love. It's a shock to everyone. No one understands."

The scene had been secured and declared off-limits until noon on Sunday. I don't know when they took Med away. I do know that the police officers asked his family to look in his room and around the house to see if he'd left a letter or a clue pointing to suicide. Nothing. Everyone agreed that he'd been was a boy brimming with life.

Two days later, the first police officer came to our house. On a Sunday afternoon. Detective Sergeant Racicot, according to the business card he left for us. An investigator. He asked a ton of questions about Med. About us. Then he told my mother that there was a psychological counselling service available to me, should I need it. I shook my head. No, I didn't want it. My mother thought that it would help. That's what she told the officer. In a shipwreck, you hold onto anything that floats.

On Monday morning, Detective Sergeant Racicot came back with another officer, this one in uniform. His name was engraved on a pin on his shirt: F. Lépine. I was fascinated by his gun. A real one. A woman was also with them, a psychologist named Éliane Lamarre.

"We'd like to speak to your son." They were not smiling. Only the woman had given me a quick empathetic smile when our eyes met, before she looked down. She seemed sympathetic. Calm.

The police asked me to sit at the kitchen table. It was topped with a laminate whose manufactured patterns of knots and grain were repeated at equal distances across the imitation wood. The psychologist also sat down with the policemen. No one was taking notes. That struck me as odd so I asked them why. "We just want to talk." My mother remained standing, leaning on the counter facing me.

They wanted me to tell them what Med and I had done during the day on Friday. The times as well, if possible, with all the details I could remember. I did my best. When I was done, Sergeant Racicot told me that several people had seen us together that day, and he wanted to know if we'd gone to the railroad together late that afternoon.

I explained that we'd already gone a few days earlier and that other friends had joined us, and told the whole story about the nickels we'd flattened into quarter-sized coins. He raised his eyebrows in amusement and told me that they'd found a few of them around Med's body. I told him that we'd planned to go back there on that fatal Friday.

"Where were you at 5:00 o'clock?"

"I don't know exactly, but I was delivering my newspapers and stopped to talk on the street with my friend Arielle for a pretty long time, and then I came back here after."

My mother added, "He was here when I got home at 5:20."

"How do you feel about what happened to your friend?" the psychologist asked.

"It seems like it isn't true… I can't really believe it… We went to play at the sandpit all morning and now my friend isn't here anymore…he's dead. I'll never see him again. It's like I'm going to hear him come down the driveway on his bike."

My vision had gotten blurry and I wiped my eyes with the back of my fingers. My mother came to me and combed a hand through my hair to smooth it down. Probably mostly out of affection or empathy, I thought. I didn't fully understand. But it reassured everyone and it made sense, under the circumstances.

Some of the actions we take serve no purpose. Sometimes doing nothing makes no sense.

They left as they had arrived. The psychologist gave my mother her card and the two of them spoke in whispers, privately.

"Where does your friend Arielle live?" the sergeant asked on his way out.

"4420 Rue des Franciscaines," I answered.

I knew her address by heart, as I did all the addresses on my paper route. Her doorbell didn't work; it was broken and you had to knock on the window to the right of it so that someone would hear. But I didn't tell them that.

My mother thumbed through the phone book to confirm the exact address. Arielle Murphy. Daughter of Pierre Murphy.

As she closed the door, she said that she thought I should see the psychologist again.

"Yeah, Mom, okay."

I think that set her at ease.

The funeral was held Tuesday morning. In an unfamiliar part of the city. In actuality, it was a burial. I saw some of our friends from school. Luc and Sam were there. We had no idea how to react or how to behave. I had been the last one to see him alive and that granted me a certain power: that of remaining silent and being the most deeply affected. People stared at me.

His family had not been able to claim the body until Monday afternoon because of the investigations and sample-taking.

According to prevailing gossip and the media, concern about his death persisted. The police wanted to get to the bottom of it. Society's demand for results. Especially in the case of a child. The previous evening, on Pierre Pascau's radio show, I'd heard an interview with Detective Sergeant Racicot. He couldn't reveal everything because an investigation was under way. "Some of it doesn't add up, so we're looking into it," he'd said.

That was the first time in my life that I knew someone who was on the radio. I was impressed by this fact. But I wondered if it was truly he, the same man who had come to my house.

Muslim ritual demands that everything be done quickly. Not like my grandfather's funeral, which after a delay of several days, had included four long days to view the body at the funeral home, followed by an interminable Catholic service, which came to an end with the burial of the coffin. Nine days after his death. Flowers and well-dressed people. Tired, too, from preserving death and drawing it out.

For Med, a hole. At the bottom of it, an almost human shape in a white sheet. The head and body turned toward Mecca. There we were, gathered around a grave, listening to prayers in Arabic not a word of which we understood but whose solemn tone reminded me of the prayers at my grandfather's interment. With tears and weeping. At one point, silence. Med's father bent down, took a handful of earth and threw it onto his son's body. A second and a third. Followed by his mother, his sisters, other family members and friends. Another silence. I walked forward to throw in three handfuls of dirt, as they had. With my mother, who was crying like a lost soul. By the end, the white sheet had disappeared. Buried underground.

The rest of the summer went by in slow motion. We all kept to ourselves. Subdued by some sort of awkwardness.

Except for a vigil in Med's memory, held the Friday after he died, which echoed images of spontaneous public tributes. Alongside the train tracks, with flowers, candles, letters, drawings and a stuffed animal. We would never speak of it again after that day.

For one of the very few times of our life, we all yearned for September and the return to school. Parents and children alike. A deep-rooted grief had settled in. Emptiness, too. We missed Med. The daily and total reality of our lives had shifted. Lives we'd believed to be uncomplicated. The lives of children. Ripped from their orbit and hurled in another direction. Into the real world and its emotions. The hours and days seemed the same, but they were tinged with a gravity that we hadn't understood until then. A head start on life experiences that we could have lived without.

I didn't speak to Arielle again throughout the whole month of August. Simply met at the funeral, once again at a store, and on the street as I was delivering newspapers. I knew that I had to thank her.

A week before school started, I set our two snakes free by turning the wooden box upside down. They didn't move. Undoubtedly comfortable with their captivity. Unaware of their freedom. Were they better off in confinement? I almost smiled at that. By nightfall, they were gone. Or they might have been eaten by a crow, I thought.

On the last Saturday of vacation, I went with my mother to buy school supplies. I hated when we had to go, list in hand, and play hide-and-seek with scholastic materials. Canada notebooks with 48 pages, eight Berol HB pencils, a Lepage glue-stick, a protractor, coloured folders, a pencil sharpener… I never figured out how my mother managed to find it all. I had an obsessive fear of the occasion. It was a big stressor in my life. I wonder if this is how suffering is eased and how mourning helps subdue the horror: a state of anguish that follows a state of shock. And so on, until the next one.

I remember thinking that Med was lucky not to have to buy everything on the list that year. I was going to share that with the psychologist. I was certain that she'd like that reaction.

Éliane Lamarre came to the house once a week. My mother attended the first two meetings because she'd taken some time off work after the incident. So that she could be near me. The third week of August, when we normally went on vacation, she went back to work. It was understood. The psychologist would come anyway. She had reassured my mother about the one-on-one meeting with me. I was nervous. Strangely, and even though she remained silent throughout, my mother's presence had been a comfort. Although the shrink seemed to want to help and was empathetic, I saw her as an enemy. I didn't know why. I believed she wanted to push me toward my emotions. I learned a lot from that first private meeting. So, because of my fear of feelings, I resisted putting a name on things. I now know that her home visits were meant to make me feel comfortable. Secure. Unsuspecting. The summer of 1981, I learned, luckily and violently, to trust my own instincts. Which from that moment on, have yet to fail me.

The first face-to-face visit proceeded in the usual fashion. I pretended to be nervous and cried a few tears to reassure her, and I talked a lot about missing my friend and about his disappearance from my life. I could tell that she liked it when I talked about the void left by Med. I paused in the middle of sentences when I told her everything we had done since the end of the school year. Éliane Lamarre was very pleased when I appeared vulnerable and fragile. I saw it in her eyes. It corresponded with her expectations and it followed the customary stages of grief. When I made repentant confessions about our stupid idea to smash coins on the railroad tracks, I burst into sobs, surprising myself with the strangeness of the big, hot tears that ran down my cheeks. She told me to let it out, that it would do me good and that it was normal. I was proud that I'd been able to cry at that exact moment and that I'd found this outlet. Inside, I missed Med, for real, but I wasn't sad at all.

The following week, when we were alone once again, she asked more questions than usual. More insistently. As if we knew each other. A familiarity too strange to be genuine.

She wanted particulars about that last day, information closer to the truth. She often repeated the same questions in different ways and wanted to know what we had talked about that morning and the night before. How had Med and I left it when we went our separate ways before noon? Why hadn't we watched *Race to Witch Mountain* together that afternoon? She insisted on telling me about Med's death in great detail. That's how I knew that there was an investigation: his arms had been cut off by the wheels of the train. Normally, she said, if he'd fallen by accident, he would have had the time to raise at least one of his arms to try to protect himself before hitting the ground. Med had fallen flat, his arms alongside his body. His arms severed at the same time as his torso.

Éliane Lamarre paused. I looked down at the ground. I stared at her feet and at her handbag, which she'd left on the floor. Seconds ticked by.

At one point, because of the angle of her handbag – its zipper not fully closed – and a ray of sun, I noticed a bluish reflection, the glint of something dark and metallic. A handgun.

She was a police officer.

I gave nothing away. I was proud that I'd been able to control myself. A few seconds later, I was choked with sobs and trembling like a leaf. She consoled me, almost as a mother would. Just that once. I shook convulsively and couldn't speak until I caught my breath. I told myself that given what she'd just told me, my reaction was entirely justified.

In crisis. Verging on hysteria. I screeched that I missed Med, that life was unfair. Sounds barely comprehensible, uttered between gasps. None of this was possible. My friend was not dead. Unreal. I would never get over his death.

A few minutes later, I'd calmed down. Actually, I let her believe that she was the one who had comforted me. She hugged me again and I remember feeling her breasts pressed against me. That had its effect on me, a stirring of desire.

Then she called my mother to tell her that I'd had somewhat of a breakdown. And I, reassuring but still a bit sad, told my mother that I was okay and that everything would be fine. I would stay quietly at home, reading comic books in my room until she returned at the end of the day. Officer Éliane Lamarre left with the promise to come back the following week. "Things will get better, Marc, you'll see." I closed the door behind her, served myself a bowl of vanilla ice cream with lots of maple syrup, and turned on the TV.

The cop-shrink kept coming back until classes began again. I never told my mother that she was a member of the police force. It would have worried her too much and there'd already been enough emotions for one summer.

School started. We were all back together for the first time since our friend had died. It was a bit weird. A shared, silent malaise. We didn't know how to move forward.

I thought it curious that things could go on this way. With no specific instructions.

The days passed and Med's absence almost became normal. I went back to hockey and homework. We paid him tribute in the school gym on Tuesday, September 22. In front of the whole school, I read a text that I had written. It was only natural that I speak. And a box filled with photos, letters and drawings was given to his family. We talked about him less and less, wanting to be somewhere else, to turn the page. Adults who were at a loss for words said that "life goes on." On the evening of September 21, just before that final ceremony, the police report was made public on the radio. An accident. Sometimes life finds a way to make sense.

I ran into Arielle that day, as I was finishing my newspaper route. At her house, at the end of the day, at 4:40 p.m.

"Did the police come see you this summer, after Med?"

"Yeah. I told them that you'd been here, with me, until 5:15 that afternoon. That you'd left so you'd be home before your mom, in time for her birthday party."

"Thanks."

I'd found her prettier than ever. I took my time going home. I also remember that the train whistled at exactly 5:02 p.m. on that second day of autumn. As usual.

I still have a photo of Med and me, side by side, taken in May of that spring. We smiled proudly. Behind us, my mother's magnolia, in bloom.

THREE

For 15 years, I have talked to flowers.

The magnolia blooms. End of April. Always at the end of April.

This shrub impressed me. As a child, I could never understand how a tree could flower before it had leaves. Later, at my own home, I would have one. The blooms lasted two weeks. Then the big heavy white flowers fell one by one, and the little tree sprouted leaves. Early May. Just as the apple trees were turning white. The season of colours and scents. Everywhere. Roots had also fascinated me since childhood. They're buried underground, tranquil and hidden. Essential. Even if we don't see them. I grew up with that tree.

I have always needed milestones. Beginnings and ends. I divided up my entire life according to natural cycles. They put my mind at ease. The light that varied. The seasons. Christmas music in December, especially John Lennon's song "Happy Xmas (War Is Over)." The smell of suntan lotion in July. The perfume of flowers. The aroma of corn cooking. Even Arielle's periods served as bookmarks.

That was what, more than anything else, I missed about her. That natural invariability. A rhythm set by nature. A woman's cycle. Like memories. Each cycle a promise, then a hope dashed. Reassuring recurrences. Evidence that the days exist. Landmarks along the way. The paths of time. A permanence.

Like a train schedule. Like the persistent dream that I still have to this day, in which all the trains arrive on time, pass before me, and fall into a ravine because the rails have been cut over the empty space. They pile up somewhere at the bottom. One day, the heap will be visible. There will be one last train. Until then, I watch them disappear, with the same fascination.

Arielle and I spent the summer we were 12 together. A year had passed since Med's death. He was gradually becoming a memory. I had largely abandoned the boys who'd been my friends. The previous summer had turned our lives upside down and avoiding each other was the easy and perhaps even the proper thing to do.

Arielle filled all their roles. I did the same things with her that I'd done with them, but there was more to it because she was a girl. We made a conscious effort not to ask ourselves too many questions.

Every evening, we knew that the next day we'd be together. No need to make plans. We would find each other. If one of us came late, if I had hockey practice, if she went shopping with her mother or went riding, whatever. We never worried about the other one. We picked up exactly where we'd left off. The grown-ups were touched by our relationship. I think we did them some good. Especially the ones who were dissatisfied with their own significant other. With reality.

With her, it was easy and normal. I have missed that since she, too, died.

Sometimes, a word or phrase rises to the surface. Out of nowhere. I adore those moments when, from out of left field, memories re-emerge. No need to understand.

"My mother really isn't too bright. This morning, she called 911 because a woodpecker was hammering away at the wall behind the house."

I understood. No questions asked. No expectations. We picked up where we'd left off. It could explain hours. An interruption. An absence. She was right: her mother wasn't smart. Arielle was the devoted and possible proof that a daughter is not necessarily like her mother.

We were also at that age where kids tend to size adults up. Those troubling insights were our first disappointments. Reality had hit us hard the previous summer.

She and I built ourselves a world apart. To combat the impending seconds and the coming years, which we suspected of being an illusion. We hated the future. We had sensed and anticipated the brokenness of adulthood. When we got rid of our misconceptions, we saw – our parents. Their inconsistencies, and the incongruity of the dreams that they sometimes shared with others, aided by wine and beer and disillusioned by their own pretensions.

We learned early on not to have expectations.

There'd be nothing more. Everything was already there.

Later, as young adults, Arielle and I got married because of her mother, to please her: she had a cancer that would soon be terminal. She had so hoped to see her daughter married and content. That was her definition of happiness. Arielle's mother was not terribly astute. Nothing serious, average in terms of her vapidity: few delicate emotions, some commonplace ideas, and lots of TV series and soap operas. A substitution: television serving as short-term treatment for social and spiritual discomfort. Passive. The vacuity that we watch.

Arielle's father, a nice if unremarkable civil servant, accepted his wife for who she was. He seemed to have a bit more substance, but nothing more than that. His grandparents had come from Ireland, which explained Arielle's red hair and freckles. Years later, when we were young adults, she became incensed whenever I called her "my little mermaid." She looked so much like Disney's animated character.

Although the real story, which dated from 1836, bore some resemblance to us, her father had not known about Hans Christian Andersen when he insisted on naming his daughter Arielle on the day she was born. He had paced the halls of the maternity ward, full of pride and wondering what he would call her. His daughter, sprung from his wife's belly and born a redhead. Arielle, he thought. A first name that he would eventually come to forget.

I always addressed him as Mr. Murphy, even when dementia had erased his past. A simple man. Unassuming. With a few tiny specks of lucidity here and there.

Although I sometimes noticed that his eyes and actions revealed a certain apprehension or embarrassment, he still appeared to love his wife, despite her limitations. Enough to last a few decades, satisfied, or so he seemed, with her. Or he did an admirable job of pretending. Which, from my point of view, was likely and worthy of mention. I have long marvelled at those who pretend to have a life, especially those whose life is miserable but who still continue to smile. And those who drink, without a second thought, to get through the lies and deceptions, have my utmost admiration.

One day, I was caught off-guard, suddenly realizing that I envied Arielle's parents. I wished I could, if only for an hour, perceive things differently. From where I sat, their lives seemed so much easier than mine. Less darkness, fewer torments. A daily life governed by a schedule. A well-defined job. Saturdays and Sundays off. An outing from time to time. Three weeks of vacation every year to go camping, planned 12 months in advance. A few sick days. The same good wishes repeated every New Year's Day.

Arielle's parents were believers. With a simple, working-man's piety that I envied: being able to trust in something bigger, something that brought an end to some of the turmoil. In a succession of relatively peaceful years. Until the end. Waiting for your demise as if waiting for someone you've agreed to meet.

And so we got married in the Catholic Church. For them. In all sincerity. It felt awkward. When we talked about it, the two of us smiled. Clear-sighted. Arielle and I, we'd made our promises elsewhere. The priest believed us.

"Thanks, Marc," she'd whispered when we turned back toward the people in the church and kissed in front of them.

I was honestly overjoyed. To be making others happy. Reception in a community hall. Her mother had organized everything. I never stopped hating her, even though I understood her limitations and good intentions. She was not particularly enlightened and her emotions were phoney. But she was Arielle's mother and she was glad to see her daughter married before she died.

But when my mother-in-law passed away, after having exasperated her family and the entire planet with her discontent and her disease, and having proudly dragged her misery all the way to the grave, I felt no emotion and had no intention of pretending otherwise. I remained a spectator, behind the scenes, detached. I hugged her father, and that was my one human gesture, the only time I'd done so since we'd known each other. It happened in a different hospital corridor, the one for the dying, just after his wife had passed away in an ugly, soulless room. With the single trace of beauty sitting in a plastic cup, a daisy that I had plucked from a flower bed across from the hospital's paid-parking lot. No one would be so bold as to plant flowers at a parking lot, I thought, and risk the loss of parking spaces and revenue. I sometimes imagine things as being worse than they are. And sometimes I surprise myself. Her father didn't hug me when his daughter died a few years later. He'd already begun to lose his wits. Nothing serious, but I did notice. A family member brought him to the ceremony. In fact, to this day I have no idea whether he was aware that Arielle had died. I sometimes envied him.

All I remember about the funeral of Arielle's mother is the flowers. Pretty and nicely arranged. A thousand scents from the bouquets and wreaths.

The same priest who had married us a few months earlier. I think he made a connection between the two events

in his funeral oration: we live with both beauty and horror…
It's God's will… His way of testing us.

I wasn't listening and was surprised when suddenly it was over. The people stood, comforted. Life went on.

Despite my lack of emotions, normal life had almost always enchanted me. Sometimes it even seemed accessible. I thought that I'd come to understand it. Like that story about the daisy. I envied others their ability to be charmed by little gestures. That too, I had learned. Deficit and desire are wonderful motivators in life.

Daily life is full of clues. All year long, we're told what we must do to be kind and sympathetic. It's a simple thing to act out the appropriate, expected behaviours. The signs are there, easy to decipher. And even easier to put into practice.

One day when we had been together for a few years, I mentioned this to Arielle. We had made coffee in a vertical espresso maker with an hourglass shape, like the ones in cowboy movies.

"Ari, I don't really have feelings or empathy for anyone. I was born that way."

"I know, Marc. I've known for a long time."

Her composure had been soothing. I wasn't worried about the fact, only about her reaction. There were days, especially with Arielle, when we came close to reaching our limits. So many times, a word or an action or a silence could have changed everything. There were times when we invented precipices of emotions with shouting and tears. To love each other more. And so many other times when I withheld word and deed. So that we could go on. We were not like everyone else.

"I'm intense, y'know."

She stated the fact, believing she was revealing something significant. As both apology and explanation. I had understood long ago and I was there with full awareness of who she was. I said nothing in response. Responding would have taken us somewhere else.

I remember the exact dates and moments when I hadn't touched her hand. When I had discouraged a sound, a word. Not just with her but with others as well.

I know by heart several hundred moments of my life when I could have changed the course of someone's destiny. A glance, a sign, a caress. Thoughts supressed. A hug withheld. Desires checked. For propriety's sake.

Arielle said nothing more. She knew who I was. "One more reason to love you," I'd said with a smile. I had assumed, wrongly, that this declaration would comfort me. Wishful thinking. Since we were little children, we had celebrated the truth. We were told that it was a moral value, a virtue. I wanted to kiss her; it was the right time. The heavens proclaimed her beauty.

I waited for the emotion. But I felt nothing. Nothing had changed inside me. Disappointed by this confession. I had spoken its name, and imagined this moment as a revelation. I waited for years. To tell her. The anticipation had been more beautiful than the declaration itself.

To tell her what I was. To stop carrying this weight. An overwhelming burden. I had been mistaken and I found it amusing. A true delight. Or some sort of consolation. Life was proving me right. Finally. Reality was not as beautiful as the dream.

No salvation. I had remained the same.

Through someone else. For whom a crack was nothing to fear. For whom a ravine would not be the end of everything. We are not always obliged to go the bottom of the abyss.

"There are some questions you just can't ask, okay? Because of the truth."

"Okay."

With that settled, we went forward. She and I became more serious. We carved out a path. Her mother was dead and her father, finally overcome by advanced-stage dementia, was placed in a care centre. We went to see him every other Sunday. Arielle left the place devasted. I went with her, fascinated by the bodies mutilated by the years, lost in old age yet still with a little life left in them. But utterly useless. In a rocking chair, standing in a hallway or lying in a bed. Worn out. No longer serving any purpose. Vacant eyes. Bodies waiting for death. Forgotten by their own memory. Stripped of their awareness by the interminable final hours.

Each time we went, I wondered why they were kept alive. And I envied them a little.

"Arielle, you had pistachio on April 18th, May 13th, May 16th, 23rd and 29th. And again on June 2nd, 9th and on the 11th too."

I always had a knack for remembering. In my mother's belly, that vessel, nature gave me an advanced degree in time. Configuration of the mind. I have an extraordinary memory.

And the words to tell. It was June 19. She was standing at the ice cream counter on Saint Lawrence, and she was hesitating. It made me smile. I know that we don't reinvent ourselves. The server was waiting for her to make up her mind. She smiled at me, impatient but with good reason.

Arielle tried to explain to her that I had just reeled off the correct dates, but the girl couldn't have cared less. She just came forward, leaned into the freezer and started to scrape some pistachio into a cone, which she handed to Arielle without waiting for her to choose.

We left without saying a word. We walked all the way home, eating our ice cream.

"Marc, I'd like us to write something together."

"Okay."

We exchanged a text for almost a year. Back-and-forths. She wrote, I read, and went on writing. I wrote and she latched onto my continuation. And I to hers. No rules. We were allowed to destroy or erase the other's words, the only requirement being to improve and serve the story. I learned a lot about her through her words. Another story told.

From this story project was born a respect that I had never imagined. Sometimes we argued. Sometimes we praised each other. We nourished the text of our lives. And the lives of our words. We managed to merge our voices. It was called *Notebooks of a Woman in Love*. We opened with accounts of our childhoods. Our little lives, those of an 11-year-old boy and girl. It began there. A text made of memories.

The summer wore on. In the morning, we had coffee together. Sitting across from each other to stimulate conversation. She knew just what to do. I preferred silence.

"Hey, I'm talking to you."

"I know."

She insisted on drinking her coffee from a little porcelain cup that I'd made in Limoges. Every morning, the same ritual. If the cup was dirty, she washed it. I had written "I love you" at the bottom. The saucer had a heart painted in red. Use of both cup and saucer was mandatory. According to the proper procedures for serving and the rules of etiquette.

One morning, I dropped the cup on the ceramic floor.

"Do you still love me, Marc?"

"Yes, Arielle… The cup didn't break…"

"Okay… Oh, look, the blackbird is back."

Each spring, a pair of blackbirds came to build their nest in our yard. Arielle said it was always same two. She may have been right. We lived in that house for several years, but I don't think that birds live that long.

While I was touched by her interpretation of the event, the birds' return left me indifferent. To her, it was full of meaning. She often said that birds are faithful unto death.

"You believe that?"

"Yes."

She saw signs everywhere. Happy with the notion of destiny. Arielle believed that the facts of life spoke to her. All the time. Everywhere.

She saw them at every street corner and in any locale, and she linked them to her present. Song lyrics, a book, a stranger passed twice on the road, a Chinese fortune cookie. She allowed her beliefs to guide her. By connecting happenstance to occurrences, she made her own good luck. Nights with a full moon could explain a risk, a thought or a curse. Solstices served as omens and coincidences as oracles.

I suppose that it's our nature to be captivated by magic and wonderment.

When I look back and review her actions, I am convinced that she knew she was going to die. Signs were there for me. I just didn't know how to read them.

I was jealous of her awareness. It was impressive. I wanted so badly to understand my inner self on the basis of the outside world. To believe that the sky is responsible for poetry. To have the feeling that we can be guided.

Convinced that this would help me move forward. Sometimes, though rarely, I was able to tolerate myself. But in general, it was always just as hard to be on the periphery of my own life. Nothing special, but in actual fact, I was much more complicated than Arielle.

I lived, for the most part, a life of avoiding myself. To survive.

The summer flowed gently by. Her last summer. Arielle. We had planted a vegetable garden. She watched over it as she would a treasure. Every morning, after coffee, she went out to do the weeding. She spent an hour a day, on her knees, pulling the weeds out. Staking the plants. Harvesting.

"Marc, a raccoon trampled your corn stalks."

The corn, and various other plants, belonged to me when she wanted me to take care of them. I prepared the Coney Bear trap, put it in a plastic pail lying on the ground and baited it with a marshmallow. It never failed.

The next day: "I caught your raccoon."

"Thanks."

In the evening, from June to October, we dined on our fruits and vegetables. Our novel-writing project had been developing nicely. "It's almost a book," I'd said in early autumn. "We just need a suicide note for the mad princess. D'you want me to write it?"

"No, it's fine, I've got it. I'll do it."

Arielle wanted to write it. The mad princess was her character, whom she'd created when we were 11. She was more Arielle's than she was mine. A princess, locked up in an asylum, so beautiful that a prince had come to rescue her by pretending to be mad himself. He then violently killed all those who'd kept them imprisoned. Arielle liked fables and phantoms. Nothing romantic here. The princess wore no gown; she gardened, went without makeup, and had dirty fingernails.

She was possessed of a fury that sometimes surprised me. Arielle Murphy carried within her all the suffering and natural violence of living. When I remember that, I smile again.

She loved, above all else, the poet Marie Uguay, to whom she was deeply devoted. To whom she also spoke, as to a ghost. Asking advice. Of her own personal ghost.

This happened to be the subject of the last painting I did in my Brooklyn studio: a portrait of Marie Uguay. For

Arielle. She'd been overwhelmed by her poetry and by the reading of her diary. One day, upon returning from the studio, I offered her the little painting, which I had secretly hung on our bedroom wall without raising any suspicion.

When she got into bed that night, she was furious with me. Silent. Not one word from the moment she took out her contact lenses until the next day.

It was a fairly academic, realistic full-face portrait of the poet, whose mouth I'd "assaulted" with white and red. Arielle cried when she came back to bed after putting on her glasses. She stared at the painting, moved and transfixed.

"I have nothing to say, okay. Go fuck yourself, Marc."

I believe that this gesture was motivated by love. Love on my part. I wanted her to be touched. I wanted her to have strong feelings and to be enchanted. I was happy when it worked. I like it when what I have in mind becomes a reality.

She took it down. And then hung it back up on the wall facing the bed so that whenever she was sitting or lying in bed, she could see it. At all times. Each night, every morning.

The portrait became a liturgy. From then on, it was a part of her life, her hopes, her day-to-day. She looked at it constantly. One day, I had tried to adjust it so that it would hang straight. She had forbidden me to touch it.

"Arielle, I'm the one who made the thing and I don't want it to hang crooked."

"Don't you touch my Marie."

Her tone was unambiguous. Threatening. Beautiful Arielle.

She got out of bed and returned it to its "crooked" position. The painting stayed like that for months. I smiled at her vigilance. Her strict supervision, as if she were the sole custodian and protector of this woman who had died too young. And of her words, which had so affected her. Arielle, the guardian. Sometimes, depending on the season, the sun fell directly on the image. A harbinger. Her day would be magical.

Each day, she touched the painting with her fingers, the way you might gently stroke a relic. To bring good luck. Or to implore.

Marie Uguay died in 1981. Arielle and I were 11 years old.

Of all the years we were in love, from a distance or in close proximity, of the more than 26 years, it was the last months that almost made me human. I spent many long hours observing her. And even longer ones picturing her in my mind.

We'd just moved in together at the beginning of our adult lives and I still had a schedule that kept me travelling everywhere and often. For my art. Getting more and more recognition. At that age, it was too late for me to switch gears. It quickly became clear that the only challenge remaining was the greatest one of all: making it last.

The duty to endure. Maintain the momentum, outlast the others. An obligation.

"Marc, I don't like it when the only news I have of you is knowing where in the world you'll be sleeping tonight."

We went to live in the country a few months later.

It had really knocked me for a loop. And started me thinking that I could settle down in one place. Go to her for good. Go back home. I tried with all my might to calm the storm. I did the best I could. I managed, I think, to put out a few fires over the years. But not the embers, buried in the ashes. Responsible for everything.

Arielle is the only woman that I have loved. I think. A situation that comes close to emotion. A kind of love that is hard to define in my case, but one that I thought about incessantly. She was the only woman I allowed inside of me. No one else has gained entry, not before her and not after.

They would have been nothing more than bit players in a foolish dream.

I thought she was beautiful. Not just the way she looked but what she did. All of it. I don't know why. And that doesn't bother me any more. I no longer try to understand why she was able to carve out a place for herself. Did she wheedle her way in with her beauty? Beauty that I mistrusted yet used to create a life that people admired.

A few days before she died, I gave her a small drawing with a two-word love note. Little more than a scrap of paper. A hand-drawn sketch. Simple. In India ink. The outline of a dahlia with dozens of petals. Done with the pen she had given me, the one that had changed my life when I'd broken my leg. She never knew that. That was what I did for her. It meant something only to me. The not telling her.

I did not speak of it at her funeral. I still have the pen and the bottle of dried-up ink. The drawing had touched her.

No, I did not speak of it. There are feelings that must remain secluded from this world.

Her eyes. Crying silent tears, sweet and warm. She had folded the piece of paper in front of me and put it in the drawer with her underwear.

Arielle planted annuals in the spring. And bulbs in the fall: perennials. I've always preferred perennials. They can live, hidden, discretely tucked away beneath the earth, and come out at will. Beautiful apparitions. During the first week of October, she had killed the grass covering a small square of earth around an apple tree by spreading a black tarp and using field stones to keep it flat when the wind blew. Stones from the earth, pushed out of the ground by the yearly frosts.

On the first Saturday in November, before the severe frosts, she worked the soil with a shovel and pitchfork and then buried her bulbs. For the following year. Columbine, lilies, tulips and peonies.

"They all have good reason to be part of our lives."

Every day, from June until the first weeks of December, she picked camomile, which she grew as much for its beauty as for the herbal tea we made in the evening.

"All my life, I've dreamt of having camomile behind my house," she said.

I have always loved flowers. I admire their sovereignty. They are beautiful for themselves alone. It's merely a coincidence in their lives that we look at them. Sometimes they are also beautiful for the birds. Have to keep an eye out for black-birds in the spring; they pluck the young sprouts just barely out of the ground. Have to give nature a helping hand sometimes.

She spent her entire Saturday planting, weeding, and recovering her garden. She died the next day, during the night between Sunday and Monday.

I have talked to flowers ever since.

That Sunday morning, Arielle had woken up before me. The sound of coffee coming through that of the rain. I stayed in bed, staring at the ceiling. I've always liked staring at the ceiling; it's such a great pleasure to let my mind wander wherever it will. I've learned a lot about myself in that private space where nothing useful seems to exist. Where I don't have to interact with anyone else. It's where I've made the biggest decisions of my life.

There was a rotating fan, like the ones in movies, and I tried to count the revolutions, with the tick-tocking of my mother's old Westclox alarm clock that had been on my bedside table since her death. Occasionally, the rotations matched the sound of the seconds passing. And then I moved on to something else. Happy to have forced coincidence onto an unexpected path. Arielle had made me a cup of coffee. With hot milk. She knew just what to do.

We went to the nursery that last Sunday. To buy more bulbs. It was raining. Her eyes were blue. We held hands. We always held hands in the car. My right hand, her left hand. The windshield wipers were making a repetitive clacking noise, a sound that I tried to synchronize with the rhythm of the music of Leonard Cohen, whom Arielle adored. I turned the wipers off and on again, hoping that they would coincide with the music. Arielle said something.

"I wasn't listening to you."

"I know… I just said that I love you, okay?"

I gave up my synchronization thing and we talked about literature. Arielle said that men who write always want to teach us something. And that they pontificate.

"Like a nervous habit."

"And women?" I asked. I knew that she was reading a book by Annie Ernaux at the time.

"Women are narcissists when it comes to their feelings. They make themselves the centre of the universe when they start thinking and writing about their emotions. But the worst, if we leave the sexes out of it, are the ones who believe literature has to lie and that it can't be violent and honest."

Then she took a swig of cold water and kissed my mouth. I drove onto the shoulder and we kissed again. Furious kisses. Her tongue was cold. It surprised me.

"This is pretty much the best day of my life."

"It's raining."

"Doesn't bother *me*."

Wild apple trees have the most beautiful flowers in all of Creation. They say that when you brew them, they cure shame and guilt. The same way drinking the morning dew on flowers is said to heal us of our regrets. Today, I know that Arielle's flowers, the ones she had planted, helped me survive her absence. Through them, I've managed to keep going, until today.

I also know that the more the distance grows between us, the more she becomes a memory. And that pisses me off.

I often find myself wishing I were the hand on a clock, fastened to the centre even though time keeps on ticking. I don't know if I loved her the way she wanted to be loved. Probably not, because I don't have the feelings that people expect. I do know, however, that I meant something to her. I believe that she truly loved me. In my heart of hearts, I stand by this perception. In fact, I know she had it too. A few weeks later, I was getting rid of her things and in her underwear drawer, right next to the little ink drawing of the dahlia, I found a USB key.

When Arielle was 11, she had all the Strawberry Shortcake dolls: Strawberry Shortcake, Apple Dumplin', Tea Time Turtle, Peach Blush, Cherry Cuddler, Mint Tulip, Hopsalot, Lime Chiffon… It was her collection of friends. Every boy in the world declared his loathing for these dolls. Secretly, we were intrigued. I remember what she told me one day as I was looking at them, all lined up on her bed, somewhat concerned because I thought it strange that she still played with dolls. She said she wanted a big family with seven kids.

"You've been warned, Marc. Take it or leave it."

When you're 11 years old, you believe whatever that age allows you to believe. Her words had affected me. I was struck by how determined she was and touched that she had chosen me to create a family with her. Life is strange. She would have seen it as a sign: Arielle died a few days after telling me that she wanted to have a child. Right away.

I'm not sure what she would have thought about this coincidence. We had never really talked about it before, aside from a few of the routine discussions between two people in love. We still considered having children to be a social phenomenon, a conformist idea, a pressure exerted by our environment. It's what young men and women are told to do. We were in our 30s and I was making a lot of money.

Without her, I would have lost my mind.

Three days before she died, she said, "I want us to make a baby." One day earlier, she hadn't wanted one, I am convinced. Something had happened. I never understood why she wanted to have a child with me. I wasn't normal.

I didn't see what she had seen.

A fraction of a second, and everything can topple over. Or right itself. This much I knew. That night, we made love without being careful. Coming inside her would no longer be a risk. My sexual release would no longer be a cause to worry. One less.

From that point on, we would leave things up to destiny.

It had been a long time since I'd had a schedule. I worked only with fury and intention. Well clear of days and deadlines. Whenever I felt like it. No calendar. Arielle looked after our daily life. She used to smile when I asked her where she was going.

"It's Monday, I'm working. Normal people work on weekdays, Marc… Bye, have a good day."

I've always hated schedules, appointments, obligations. I hated people, hated meeting them, going to restaurants, running into friends, having to talk. In public, I was incapable of holding a conversation with more than two people. My brain short-circuits. Noise is agony. I've learned to stifle my hostility and survive the situation, but it's not easy. Arielle was the only one who knew.

Generally speaking, I hated everyone. Except her. I never knew why. Arielle Murphy was the only person who managed to come near. The only person who ever accepted me as I was.

All of this had worried me a bit. I knew that I was hard to live with. Not something I was proud of. Somewhat ashamed of the fact. Making the best of a bad situation. With her, it wasn't an effort, it was a reason to live.

Her death had troubled me. I didn't feel sadness, even though I feigned thousands of tears of grief to reassure the others.

I experienced her death as a deep disquiet. The bottom of the mineshaft. A bumping post at the end of the line. There was one near the pit. Two pieces of metal that rise vertically above the railroad tracks. Nothing after. Dead end. That's as far as it goes.

Ironically, when seen from the side, these stoppers mimic the calligraphic shape of the infinity sign.

A shadowy ravine. Something had disappeared into its darkness. A strength, too. Beginning on that day in November, I decided to pretend to be normal, to be a well-adjusted, sociable guy. I had capitulated. I was going to act as if everything in the future could be orderly and marvellous. I was going to melt into the masses, blend in with crowd. Become like everyone else.

Arielle had fallen asleep as usual. Always, even after having a disagreement or getting angry, we kissed each other good-night. Even when the other one was already asleep.

That November night had been like all the rest. She curled up against me. She was always cold at night, no matter what the season.

My arm under her, her head on my chest. She never knew it, but I was never able to fall asleep until I'd synchronized my breathing with hers. She calmed me down. The only person who managed to stanch my constant flow of thoughts. The only one who managed to dam my rage.

Shortly before midnight, she abruptly woke up and barely had the time to say "I don't feel well" in a single suffocated breath. She hugged me with all her might before letting go. Her eyes turned inward. Dead. Struck down as if by lightning. I tried everything I could, all the actions we're told to take.

Her body was no longer there. Thrombosis and a ruptured aneurism. They said age had nothing to do with it. It can happen to anyone at any time. The opposite of a lottery.

Arielle had no brothers or sisters. She had no one left but her senile father, some friends, a few distant aunts and uncles, and her colleagues from work. It meant a lot to me that people came to the funeral. It was discussed by journalists, who were fascinated by our tragic destinies, "the wife of…died from a stroke…inquiry…coroner's report."

People were suddenly captivated by the human violence that had been such a big part of my artwork. As if it were a prophesy. As if it were normal. To live by the sword.

To see signs. Worse: to believe in them. As if it were acceptable that the only woman I might ever love should die in my arms. At an age when we can usually expect only to live.

One of the disadvantages of dying young is not having the chance to come to terms with death. Even though we'd grown up with a religious background and undercurrents of piety, and had learned a little from Med's death and that of our mothers, nothing since then had given meaning to this absolute darkness.

I did the best I could. The arrangements, the legal documents, the estate. A ceremony, which resembled a funeral where people talk and cry. With me, standing before a gathering of humans, telling stories and trying to turn them into a eulogy. Arielle was gone.

From then on, it was mainly because of other people's tears, and the temporary reprieve they granted me for the near future, that I obediently agreed to live an abject, well-adjusted, predictable human life. I became a citizen, a widower to some, upon whom benevolent thoughts were bestowed. A helpful and empathic man. A man whom others hoped would be granted lenience, alone as he was in his bereavement. Someone different from me. I was twofold, and contemptuous. I didn't give a damn about compassion.

I pretended to know nothing of my ill repute. It's what I do best.

I told – improvised – a story at the ceremony: I reminisced about a spinning top. Fall of 1981, after Med. A Sunday in November.

We still didn't know what should happen between us. She and I. To define our relationship and exist. We guessed at the expectations without really understanding them. Before adulthood brought us down to reality. A spinning top. The relic of another age, a gift I had received before school when I was five. I suspect nostalgic adults of repeating back to children, like echoes, the memories and objects of their own childhoods. Compensating for a loss.

We had been fascinated by my top, and for a few seconds, hypnotized. It was red and yellow. Made of metal. With white flowers that looked like daisies. When it spun, the patterns' clarity was lost. The flowers merged with the colours and became a slow and silent motion. Just the faint noise of friction and of the air whipping around it. A slight murmur. The top balanced on a point scarcely as big as the tip of a pen. It stayed there, upright, as long as it was whirling. Then it fell over, spinning a few times on its side, disoriented, before coming to a stop. The end of a cycle. We started it up again by pumping its threaded stem several times. The top regained its strength and stayed upright even longer. Then it stopped twirling once again.

I don't know why this memory has remained so vivid. I think I wanted to read into it a metaphor for love. To find meaning in this game. For two decades, I tried to use it to explain us. One day, I understood that it was about the time we spent together, observing this bit of magic, that had brought us together. The invisible, once again. Like the mysteries that we invent to keep on living. We come to believe in them and that is enough to fuel the future. What we keep telling ourselves ends up being our consolation.

We have to enjoy spinning in circles if we're to go on smiling.

I learned a long time ago that if we stay on the path laid out before us, it will take us only to a predetermined destination. I knew it at the age of 11.

After Arielle's death, I rebuilt my life as a normal man. In the beginning, it was to get my revenge. It seemed to me that this was what had to be done. I claimed to be in love. For real. By lying to everyone. As was right and proper, with promises and dreams. I even took pride in it. A wife. Children. A family. A house. Several houses. In several countries. A career that continued to grow in meaning and earn more respect. Friends. Smiles. Vacations. With the future still ahead of us. To prove that I was like everyone else. With narcissistic conviction.

But always without appetite. For anything. I pretended that I was happy. I did a good job of pretending that I was happy. I did it so well that for a number of years, I sensed that people were jealous of me. I found it oddly funny, being envied for my sham of a life. It only fuelled my contempt.

And this with the mourning of Arielle hovering in the background. Grief off in the distance, wandering astray. A delayed reaction, but as searing as a burn. Always. A sorrow without end. Astronomical. Perceived, sometimes, as a fracture. A dull pain, a phantom affliction. Like when you realize your leg is broken: the body acts as if the pain isn't where it actually hurts. The body pretends it's somewhere else. It takes off for a different place. Everywhere and nowhere at the same time.

And so I swallowed back my furies. Those that perpetuate life and those that set boundaries. Telling myself that it was good for my art. And for the beast that I am. For such a long time, we have chosen to believe that suffering motivates us. We adore martyrdom, tragedies, dramas, and the accompanying emotions. Pale substitutes for freedom.

We like to believe that windmills transform wind into flour. And we invent them, too, sometimes, however useless they may be. That's human nature. Why not railroad tracks as well? Seems to me that we transport copious amounts of feelings, more of them than we actually work through. One track, two women. A freight train with no fireman. Billions of consciousnesses in a convoy with no rails.

How I wished that some people would live. And that others would die. I often wish that some of the people I know would die.

I strangled too many things for so many years. Thus far. Until now. Slaughtered so much beauty. I whispered my violence into the art I made. Don't be a narcissist. Don't be a narcissist. Do not be a narcissist. Control that "other." Hide him from others. So that life can go on, again. Follow the lifeline. Find the tomorrows within yourself. That impossible future. So that people won't be afraid of me.

At a very early age, I realized that a race protecting its weakest members is destined to fail. Even when that race realizes what it's doing, apologizes and gets itself organized. Even when repentant and historical. Its cycles, like miscarriages. An unnamed beauty in its decline. Which we repeat and prop back up like a top. For as long as it lasts.

I am not a believer, and yet every day of my life I prayed, before the flowers, to be nothing more than an animal in love.

I had harnessed my nature and made it a thing of wonder. Art exposes us and lies to us, in proper and terrifying proportion. I learned to say "I love you" when it mattered. Everyone believed me. In the right place and at the right time.

I also learned to say "I love you" at the moments when it's least expected. Those instances count even more. I continued to shed tears at the appropriate intervals, and in front of the right people. I freed myself from the silence. I seemed to know how to communicate, and I was able to identify the difficulties and any number of suppositions.

Since Arielle's death, I've managed to supress all my urges to kill people. It would serve no purpose, as I keep telling myself. The problem lies elsewhere. Everywhere. I smile when I hear the clarion call of love and note its mission to exist, providing both proof and condemnation of one's self. Simultaneously. Life is right here. It is manifold, and these multiple lives exist within us. Some gasp for air, and others cry out. Love is the most egocentric emotion in the Universe. The most autistic, too.

And so I tested the waters. I went to sleep every night, telling myself that I had good reason to try. I tried very hard. I wanted to believe in the standard moral values: mutual support, generosity, justice, family, the right to hope and dream. Telling myself all the while that I wouldn't be disappointed. I almost signed on to the project. I truly gave it a chance.

To no avail.

I woke up every morning for years on end, anesthetized by a burning faith and a clear-headed cruelty, and certain that there was a destination. But always with the sad suspicion that life was going nowhere. I tamed the fury. For a little while. And then a little while longer. The years piled up in the abyss. You have to love the ugliness to find the beauty.

I sincerely hoped that participation in the whole adventure would make me believe in it. Telling myself that by dint of having been part of it, I would eventually be convinced. Buying stuff, consuming, wanting. Dreaming, too; they say it's good to have dreams. They heal and soothe. Dreams are absolutely necessary because having them reassures us. And it comforts others when we describe them in detail. It makes things seem real. Normal.

Since her death, I have lived with her ghost. Arielle. Long, lovely years. Difficult in the beginning. The loss of her physical presence. I managed to adjust and accept it. I still talked to her. And she still helped me, as did my mother. In all things. A great deal, artistically speaking. But in particular, she gave me memories and the strength I needed to smile from time to time. And to keep acting as if everything was all right.

At first, I swore to myself that I would never love again. Incapable. Despite the breach opened by Arielle, who entered through a crack. And then a crevice. Too often, I am merely a ravine.

The spring after she died.

The snow had melted. The crocuses always come up first. Snowdrops, they're called. They arrive with the crows.

Then come the wild daisies and the starlings. The magnolia. And all the others follow. With the tulips. The flowers rise out of the soil. The blackbirds return. Second week of May.

I was awakened by the strident cries of the swallows defending their nests and by those of the Canada geese in the sky, calling down to Earth to verify their route. Geese know where to go. Far away. They know where they're going. Or so it seems. There is an order, even if it repeats itself and goes around and around in circles.

I hadn't had a sip of coffee since the previous autumn. Could not do it. Sometimes, memories are an affront. That Tuesday, I felt the urge. While the machine heated up, I went outside to gather a bouquet, instinctively. Long stems. Flowers plucked by hand. A makeshift bouquet with dandelions and lilacs. Bursting with colour. I put the flowers in an empty wine bottle. A day verging on normal. Maybe, just maybe, a future. I don't remember smiling, but it was almost as if I had. It was in this spirit that I found the courage to sort through and get rid of Arielle's belongings.

I remember inhaling deeply to smell all of her clothes before folding and piling them up. Especially her lingerie. Seeking her odours. Seeking her. Arielle, the woman. Reconnecting a bit. Sensory memory. One more time. Without the reality of her. Everything smelled of lavender: dried flowers in a sachet, kept under her clothes.

I know that it's impossible to make thoughts and memories disappear. But the objects attached to them, you can. I put her things into cardboard boxes. When I ran out of boxes, I put her stuff into garbage bags. So that I could give them away to charities. I would go at night. Leave them in some anonymous donation bin at the town's community centre when no one would see me. So that I wouldn't have to look people in the eye and explain where it all came from. I had drawn hearts on the boxes with a black felt-tip pen. And the initials A.M. Everything was neatly folded.

It was a simple thing to do. Open the cover, drop in the boxes and bags, make a ritual of it. I went back eight nights in a row. On the afternoon of the ninth day, I locked eyes with a woman through the window in the public library's door. A stranger. She looked at me, gave a scarcely noticeable nod of her head, and said nothing. I knew that things would work out. I could make them work out. So I persevered. Running on empty.

That unknown woman never knew of the courage she had given me.

Buried at the bottom of the top drawer: notes, letters, shells, a few of my drawings that I had given her, jewelry from her mother, a photograph, and a USB key. I remembered. Her drawer. A place for safekeeping.

I spent the rest of that day and night, and the next three weeks, reading and rereading Arielle. She had written short stories and poems. Three completed novels. Notes and plans for four others. The intimacy of her writings. I grew very attached to her words. They helped me, a little, to make peace with her absence. I discovered, through her words, all the beauty of her female ferocity.

A memory. One evening, several years ago. We had just moved in together. At summer's end. In a park. Swings, which we loved. We saw the city's glowing lights reflected on the clouds and on the river.

"You're sure I'm the one you want? I'm high maintenance, y'know…"

"I know."

I remember her face when she was happy. I had learned. I kept silent. No word could have properly translated or described that look. I believe that Arielle knew how to keep me alive. In spite of herself.

Without her, I'd cease to exist. I never did have any sort of intuition. Yes, of course, I had a bit of instinct, which is in fact nothing but a fraction of a second of a head start on the present. I don't know how I came to have it. I was born lucky, I guess.

She taught me about flowers. Without them as well, I would've called it all quits. Then everything became a secret. A memory. I often find myself imagining that she's still here. Sometimes I think that she has an even greater presence that way. From somewhere else. Like a church bell that has slipped the bonds of its beliefs but continues to ring, as an act of mercy and for the memories. I remember the desire in her eyes. Her frontier. The imperative to love each other, here, now. This woman's present moment was the most beautiful.

November. A few days before her death, breathless, she said, "My maternal grandmother recited her rosary every day."

"Mine did, too, and she died in her vegetable garden one autumn while she was digging up potatoes the way it's done there, only it was during Mass. The only time of year, during the harvest, when she didn't go."

"You know why I love you, Marc?"

"Uh…no."

"Because."

"I love you, too, y'know, even if I get it all screwed up sometimes."

She let a few seconds pass and then said, "Marc… I just want to tell you… I never wanted, or planned, or hoped to come out of this unscathed."

I drove the pitchfork deep into the soil with one foot, sometimes jumping on it with both feet together to gain a few centimetres of depth, and I forced the earth to come up and turn over. The potatoes appeared. Arielle bent down and I stole a glance at her breasts, which I could see through the open neck of her shirt and checkered jacket. My blood rushed.

She gathered the potatoes and put them in a crate made of woven strips of wood. For the winter. We stored them in a cool place to have for the rest of the year. That episode remains, to this day, the most romantic moment of my entire life as a man. We were going to go far, she and I. At last. Working the land together. Mapping out our time.

We might just go the distance, I'd thought. Six months later, I recognized her brassiere while emptying out her drawer. White. Woven like the basket. "Macramé," I'd said with a smile, the first time she'd unhooked it in the urgency of love. That time, I had come on her breasts. I remember her eyes, closed. And her smile.

Memories attach themselves as much to things as they do to us, in order to survive. They need our lives. I have always kept, in a little box of mementos, a flattened nickel from that summer when we were kids.

The years passed. I often caught myself thinking of her. But the present lay elsewhere. With a different woman. I would have loved to find the strength to forget. And when I had to struggle against the onslaught of her absence, I was glad that I had no feelings. Everything is easier when you've escaped your emotional chains. Having no feelings. Being afraid of feelings. Being panic-stricken by your feelings.

I believe that nature made a flower for me. It disconnected me from the awareness of existing. I was born derailed.

After Arielle, I shut myself up in the studio for months. People kept their distance, convinced that I was grieving.

Safe from others. I spent one whole year painting nonstop, creating works both violent and beautiful. No particular intention. Going with the flow. I read her words. The ones she'd left behind. In a never-ending spiral. Toxic. Magnificent and morbid at the same time. As if the two were irrevocably linked. A deadly dance. We will never fully understand that instinct: to love and hate with the same ferocity. Energy diverted.

Arielle passed through my life like a dream. Too quickly and then she was gone. Since then, I've been afraid of memories. I'm afraid that I'll forget her. Sometimes, in the midst of social pleasantries and among people who are busy congratulating, or detesting, or envying me, I keep my cool and go on listening or at least pretend to, but I'm actually thinking of her. I have a memory that can outlast time: foolproof and infallible. Life works things out for the best: my brain tunes people out when they speak to me. A most fortunate state of affairs.

I often missed the big moments but I have no regrets. It was the thousands of small acts and minuscule events that, in the end, bound us together. But the evidence eludes me. Like words on a page, it is often the white spaces between the sentences that define me. The further I get from Arielle with the passing of time, the more human I become.

I seem to remember one first day of May, a few years after her death, when I cried for the first time in my life. As if I had emotions. All of a sudden. It hadn't even come as a surprise.

The crying of tears had been preceded by a feeling, muted as it was, and this was normal.

Normal for me, the one who had always believed that art sought to define us. When, on the contrary, it reflects only a yearning for what isn't there. It echoes the emptiness.

Arielle's words and stories taught me, her somewhat reluctant student, so much about her. I still talk to her, every day, ever since. I take care not to say her name out loud. It would send out too many shock waves. And cause too much confusion. She and I were married beneath the roots. Normal life grew above us.

"Check out my breasts, they're swollen and sensitive… I said to myself, 'Marc will think they're beautiful.'"

She had smiled and taken off her bra, then asked me to touch them. That was the last of our lovemaking. "I need your hands on me, I love your hands…" We made love to each other. As if to battle the passage of time. To tell it to fuck off.

"What're you doing tomorrow?"

"Good night, Ari."

"Marc… What're you doing tomorrow?"

"Gonna go count the stars and make an atlas. One day we'll find our way and the two of us will be free."

"I don't get any of that, but I think it's beautiful… G'night. I love you, 'kay?"

We held each other tight, the windows open to November, the night air on our cold, hot skin. Her womanly odours under the covers. I matched my breaths to hers for a few minutes, and I fell asleep nestled against her sweet softness.

When I look back over the years, I think that I lied because I was terrified of the truth.

There are moments when she cannot exist. This is an unspeakable disappointment that I've had to face. I chose to make art because it is a language that appeared to me unfiltered. A far cry from the one found between "I love you" and "I hate you." A language that I did not know but tried to learn.

Arielle could no longer exist. I know that now. I have no way of knowing where the two of us would have ended up. Maybe we would have had a family. Maybe we would have managed to raise children better that us. It's also possible that we crammed lies and promises down each other's throat. I made elsewhere, and with someone else, the life she and I had hoped to have together.

I overturned every belief to reach this point. Telling myself that it would be better this way. Because for as long as we can remember, we've been petrified to tell the truth. Reality is often ashamed of us.

The further we get from our true nature, the more we become one with the masses. With determination and to excess. Unless we believe in visions and angels. And in lying to ourselves.

When I squeeze red paint out of a tube, because it says "cadmium red" on the label, and cadmium red is what comes out, I am pleased. It's the little things, I tell myself. I'm going to make it. Make it to the end with as few mistakes as possible. Take the most scenic route, regardless of the risks, the cliffs, the detours, the waterfalls, the dangers and the years. We have to learn how to go around in circles. How not to be a straight line. Railroads intrigue me because they're straight lines. We have to change course.

As far back as I can recall, there were occasions when I might have wanted to be capable of love. I'm still giving myself a little time. Arielle will help me. Through all the confessions and all the misgivings that come with it. I will end up saying the words.

A few weeks ago, I painted her portrait. I will show it to no one. Not ever. Keep it far from the art market and expectations. It is for me. It had become a rare occurrence, making art just to please myself. It's not the work – the object itself – that has meaning. It's the making of it. The physical thing is secondary. I erased the eyes and started them over three times. Her hazel eyes, luminous and brimming with truths. Her eyes, which changed colour according to the weather, sometimes turning cobalt blue when it was going to rain.

"Thank you, Arielle," I wrote on the back of the painting, in ink. A testimonial. And the lifeboat that saved me.

I remember the first time I went to the Louvre. I despise travelling unless it's to visit museums. Museums preserve the past. Arielle had come to meet me.

The only reason to go on a trip. *The Raft of the Medusa* by Géricault. He painted the official story of the survivors of a political shipwreck. Painters have that power: to portray their ideas with impunity. For some, like Delacroix, that meant horses. For others, like Goya, it was the violence of human nature, and others still, like Rothko, chose spirituality.

Each time, it was the inviolability of life that was expressed.

Arielle, my horizon. The attention she paid shielded me from the burden of living. The hopes and the disappointments. Like poetry.

I often stand in the middle of my studio. Not moving a muscle. Sometimes with good reason, sometimes just lost and bewildered. I'd forgotten that the studio was such an area of freedom. A place providing immunity. Painting is an act of total honesty and of irreverence. Untamed. Unsavoury. I believe that is what she wanted of me. Foresight. With odours and meanings that are, by their very nature, reason enough to exist. Just as the scent of flowers goes hand in hand with their magic and wonderment.

Arielle pushed me to another place. Throughout all time. In every season, I detect her presence, in her cycles. All this reassures me. I like to think that she's watching, somewhere, in silence. I conjure her up everywhere.

My behind-the-scenes are truer than all the rest of it: they convey more certainties than the action on stage. To this day, I still don't know if I was in love. I do know, however, that I was on the verge of the feeling. And that is already saying quite a lot.

I vehemently owe a large part of who I am, and what my future will be, to her.

Arielle's flowers reappear each spring. So beautiful. As they have every year since we were children. Her flowers. Faithfully returning like her menses. I continued to talk to them. They embodied my bereavement. I would have loved to interrupt her periods.

I still drink camomile tea. I think of her, every time I pour the water into the teapot that she'd fashioned out of clay. I dread the day it breaks.

People thought it normal that I should cling to something in the beginning. Then one day, I became another woman's man. No one would understand. I preferred to keep quiet about it. To silence the echoes.

I often talk to her. About anything and everything. I tell her about my days, how I pass the hours. The joys as well as the sorrows. In any case, I'm certain that she always knew, without my having to spell it out. On one rare occasion, a few months ago, her absence made me sad. As if I were actually human.

I will never have the humility of a believer. Nor will I ever experience the bewilderment and anguish of such devotion. I have finally accepted the stipulations set by nature. By mine. My nature.

But sometimes, often: a shiver. Like the whistling of a train.

One morning in late summer. The house was calm and quiet. I was alone. I had gathered a bouquet of flowers, some from the garden and some that grew wild. I adore doing this kind of thing. Cutting the flowers with stems long enough to put in water. And even as I cut them, I know that they will die.

A glass jar sitting on the dining-room table. The scent is everywhere. Sometimes I think that Arielle never died or that she never existed.

"I don't want you to die, okay, I just couldn't handle it."

"I promise, Ari. I promise."

"Marc, put your hands on my cheeks."

I kept my promise. But I have often wondered what the point of all this is. I wanted so badly to fade out of the picture. Or to cover some of it up. And do better.

Each year, in spring and fall, I plant vegetables in the vegetable patch and flowers in their beds. I put things into the earth. I know that you don't have to dig down into the abyss to make things take root. To each its own depth.

Distances – even those far, far away – belong to us.

Sometimes, I touch the soil and my fingers gently find their way beneath the surface. Just deep enough. On occasion, I open it up and probe its depths with bitterness and rage. It makes perfect sense. On such days, my skins dries and cracks. The way it does in the studio.

At night, worn out, I look at the traces of dirt and of colours on my hands, and almost smile, convinced that I exist, so vivid are my memories. Upon waking in the morning, I find comfort in those traces of soil and paint on my skin.

Marc Séguin books with Exile Editions
translated by Kathryn Gabinet-Kroo

HOLLYWOOD

Marc Séguin is a master when working with events of enormous impact, and wonderfully empathetic in his revelations about the human heart. *Hollywood* is a tale full of fateful meetings and strange coincidences, and an exploration of those moments that stand against the hypocrisy of the American Dream, what many now consider an unattainable "made-in-Hollywood" ideal.

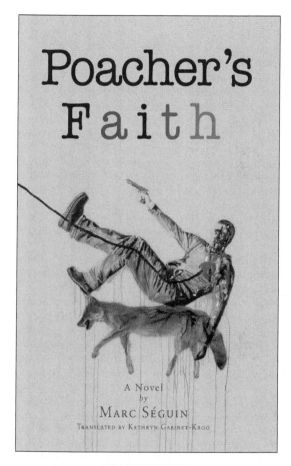

Poacher's
Faith

A Novel
by
MARC SÉGUIN
TRANSLATED BY KATHRYN GABINET-KROO

POACHER'S FAITH

Marc Morris is many things, but he is principally a hunter. Half Mohawk, half Caucasian, he is filled with a deep bitterness fuelled by disillusionment. As he himself freely admits, he kills animals so he won't kill men. And yet, he has faith – or, at least, faith in faith. The story begins on the day after Marc's failed suicide attempt, and traces back through the ten years preceding this event, during which he criss-crossed Canada and the United States, driving thousands of kilometres in his pickup to phsically trace out the giant "FUCK YOU" that he determinedly felt-tipped on his road map.

Kathryn Gabinet-Kroo books in translation
with Exile Editions

AMUN

A GATHERING OF INDIGENOUS STORIES SELECTED BY
Michel Jean

TRANSLATED BY
Kathryn Gabinet-Kroo

AMUN

"Ten different stories set in multiple epochs and contexts, offering glimpses of lives that provide a wider view and understanding of Indigenous experiences."
—*Montreal Review of Books*

"Young or old, men or women, Innu, Huron-Wendat or Métis, the ten authors of *Amun* have one thing in common…they write to a certain extent with their blood: their stories resonate with personal dramas and a memory abused by centuries of oppression…"—*Le Devoir*

PATHS OF DESIRE
Emmanuel Kattan

This is the story of a Jewish/ Muslim woman's suspense-filled journey of discovery as she confronts her family's origins, and the realities of living and loving in a turbulent environment where faith and religion are inextricably mixed with politics and daily life – all too often creating frontiers and barriers in the souls of the people.

ZIPPO
Mathieu Blais
& Joël Casséus

This is a work as frightening as it is fascinating: In a North American city in the not too distant future, a great economic summit is getting under way and Nuovo Kahid is the journalist assigned to cover it. "More than just a dark futuristic novel, *ZIPPO* sits at the rarely visited border between the detective story and science fiction."—*Solaris*